T0029292

IN THE FOG

RICHARD HARDING DAVIS

Edited, with an introduction and
notes, by Leslie S. Klinger

LIBRARY OF CONGRESS

Poisoned Pen
PRESS

Published by Poisoned Pen Press, an imprint of Sourcebooks,
in association with the Library of Congress
P.O. Box 4410, Naperville, Illinois 60567-4410
(630) 961-3900
sourcebooks.com

This edition of *In the Fog* is based on the first edition in the Library of Congress's collection,
originally published and copyrighted in 1901 by R. H. Russell. Illustrations by Thomas
Mitchell Peirce and F. D. Steele are original to the book. "Gallegher: A Newspaper Story"
was first printed in *Gallegher, and Other Stories*, published and copyrighted by Charles
Scribner's Sons in 1891. Illustrations by Charles Dana Gibson are original to the book.

Cataloging-in-Publication Data is on file with the Library of Congress.

Printed and bound in the United States of America.
KP 10 9 8 7 6 5 4 3 2 1

To
Bruce and Nancy Clark

"I cannot tell you how much I have to thank you for."

CONTENTS

FOREWORD

Crime writing as we know it first appeared in 1841, with the publication of "The Murders in the Rue Morgue." Written by American author Edgar Allan Poe, the short story introduced C. Auguste Dupin, the world's first wholly fictional detective. Other American and British authors had begun working in the genre by the 1860s, and by the 1920s we had officially entered the golden age of detective fiction.

Throughout this short history, many authors who paved the way have been lost or forgotten. Library of Congress Crime Classics bring back into print some of the finest American crime writing from the 1860s to the 1960s, showcasing rare and lesser-known titles that represent a range of genres, from cozies to police procedurals. With cover designs inspired by images from the Library's collections, each book in this series includes the original text, reproduced faithfully from an early edition in the Library's collections and complete with strange spellings and unorthodox punctuation. Also included are a contextual introduction, a brief biography of the author, notes, recommendations for further reading, and suggested discussion questions. Our hope is for these books to start conversations, inspire further research, and bring obscure works to a new generation of readers.

Early American crime fiction is not only entertaining to read but it also sheds light on the culture of its time. While many of the titles in this series include outmoded language and stereotypes now considered offensive, these books give readers the opportunity to reflect on how our society's perceptions of race, gender, ethnicity, and social standing have evolved over more than a century.

More dark secrets and bloody deeds lurk in the massive collections of the Library of Congress. I encourage you to explore these works for yourself, here in Washington, DC, or online at www.loc.gov.

—Carla D. Hayden, Librarian of Congress

INTRODUCTION

At the turn of the twentieth century, American crime fiction was at a shallow ebb. Anna Katharine Green, who had achieved great success with *The Leavenworth Case* in 1887, continued to produce popular novels (and would do so until 1923), but the tastes of American readers of mystery fiction had turned to England. Certainly the popularity of the Sherlock Holmes stories had focused attention on British crime writing, but not until Mary Roberts Rinehart, whose first novel appeared in 1908, the popular *The Circular Staircase*, did American mystery writers again achieve success.

It is not surprising, then, that Richard Harding Davis— the most popular American journalist of the day—set a work of crime fiction in London. In his novella, a visitor to London becomes lost in the fog at night and wanders into a house, where he finds two murder victims. Three different narrators tell of the adventure and the resulting investigation. Though one reviewer hailed it as a "decided innovation in 'detective' fiction,"* that was hardly the case; in fact, its charm is in evoking many of the

---

Baltimore Sun, December 19, 1901, 8.

clichés and popular settings of crime writing. Ellery Queen, the great mystery author/editor, hailed the tale as the "curtain raiser" of the first golden age of detective short-storytelling, "a perfect blend of Anglo-American storytelling."*

By the 1880s, fog had become a symbol of pervasive but hidden evil. Christine L. Croton, in *London Fog: The Biography*, observes:

> *A metaphorical relationship between social conflict and fog became apparent—a fear that the most brutal members of the residuum could spread across London, moving from east to west, like the fog, to upset the social balance and wreak havoc and destruction. In the West End disturbances of 1886, indeed, this threat for a time became a reality, further stoking the fires of social tension and anxiety.*†

The fogs of London had a special frisson for Victorian readers. Arthur Conan Doyle's Holmes stories were indelibly set, with few exceptions, in fog- and smog-polluted London.‡

---

*Ellery Queen, *Queen's Quorum: A History of the Detective-Crime Short Story as Revealed by the 106 Most Important Books Published in this Field since 1845* (Boston: Little, Brown, 1951), 46.

---

†Cambridge, MA: Belknap Press, 2015, 120. Also known as the Trafalgar Square Riots or the Pall Mall Riots, on February 8, 1886, in a clash between backers of the Fair Trade League and the Social Democratic Federation, almost 100,000 people (according to newspaper estimates) marched from Trafalgar Square to Hyde Park, smashing windows at clubs, offices, and shops along the way.

---

‡*The Hound of the Baskervilles*, published only a few months before *In the Fog*, makes much use of the fogs on the Great Grimpen Mire in Dartmoor, and although the coda to the tale takes place on a "raw and foggy night" in London, London fogs are not a plot element. It wasn't until "The Adventure of the Bruce-Partington Plans," published in 1908, that Holmes would expressly remark on the London fogs: "Look out of this window, Watson. See how the figures loom up, are dimly seen, and then blend once more into the cloud-bank. The thief or the murderer could roam London on such a day as the tiger does the jungle, unseen until he pounces, and then evident only to his victim." Arthur Conan Doyle, *Sherlock Holmes: The Complete Short Stories* (London: John Murray, 1928), 968.

Vincent Starrett, in his sonnet "221B," penned in 1942, charac-
terized the setting of Doyle's tales:

> *A yellow fog swirls past the window-pane*
> *As night descends upon this fabled street:*
> *A lonely hansom splashes through the rain,*
> *The ghostly gas lamps fail at twenty feet.*[*]

Of course, Doyle was not the only writer to immerse his
tales in fog. Charles Dickens's *Bleak House* (1853) describes
"fog everywhere. Fog up the river…fog down the river, where
it rolls defiled among the tiers of shipping and the waterside
pollutions of a great (and dirty) city." Robert Louis Stevenson's
Strange Case of Dr. Jekyll and Mr. Hyde (1886) has several scenes
set in the fog, and the theme of pollution is central to the story:
Jekyll's downfall is brought about by "impurities" in the chem
icals (as well as, of course, impurities in Jekyll himself). The
London scenes of Bram Stoker's *Dracula* (1897) are immersed
in smoke, amid fears of the "unclean."[†] Indeed, even the fog itself
could be a danger. In William Hay's 1880 *The Doom of the Great
City*, a black fog covers London for months, bringing death
and destruction. Thus Davis's evocation of a fog-shrouded city
would have immediately set the stage for a tale of shocking
crimes and characters who are not what they seem.

In the Fog was Davis's first attempt at long-form crime fiction.
His previous writing had achieved solid success but included
only a few criminous stories. For example, his collections

---

[*]Vincent Starrett, "221B (for Edgar Smith)," *Autolycus in Limbo* (New York: E. P.
Dutton, 1943), no. 32, unpaginated.

[†]These works are explored in depth in chapters three and four of Jesse Oak Taylor's
The Sky of Our Manufacture: The London Fog in British Fiction from Dickens to Woolf
(Charlottesville: University of Virginia Press, 2016).

Gallegher, and Other Stories (1891), *Van Bibber and Others* (1892), and *The Exiles, and Other Stories* (1894) dabbled in the occasional tale of robbers or grifters. Throughout his career, Davis drew on his stints as a war correspondent in the Second Boer War (in South Africa) and the Spanish-American War, both reporting on the action and fictionalizing his experiences. (Winston Churchill and Jack London were also well-known war correspondents of the era whose other writing was informed by the stories they lived and heard.) Davis's first great success, the novella *The Princess Aline* (1895), is about the adventures of a young American artist who falls in love with a picture of a European princess and travels to Europe to find her. The book was the fifth bestselling book in America in its year of publication.*

Davis set out to make fun of the genre of crime fiction. The Englishman Sir Andrew, the lynchpin of *In the Fog*, is a devotee steeped in the mysteries of the French writer Émile Gaboriau† and Arthur Conan Doyle (both specifically mentioned) as well as the countless other English and French crime writers of the day. The mystery reader was by nature an addict, Davis suggests, and certainly the bookstalls of fin-de-siècle London offered much to satisfy the addict's cravings. The quantity of pre-twentieth-century crime fiction can only be estimated. Graham Greene and Dorothy Glover, for example, were assidu-ous collectors of those titles and in 1966 published a catalogue

---

*Alice Payne Hackett and James Henry Burke, *80 Years of Bestsellers: 1895–1975* (New York: R. R. Bowker, 1977), 3.

---

†Émile Gaboriau (1832–1873) was the prolific French author of numerous mystery novels. His work was widely translated and readily available in England. His best-known creation was Monsieur Lecoq, an inspector for the Sûreté, whom Sherlock Holmes derided as a "miserable bungler" in Arthur Conan Doyle's *A Study in Scarlet* (*Beeton's Christmas Annual* [London: Ward, Lock, 1887], 14).

of their collection, consisting of 471 titles*; however, Greene freely admitted that their collection was far from complete, and he hoped that in the ten years after publication, it would double in size.†

Davis's *Arabian Nights*–like novella of three linked tales focuses on intrigues of great popularity. The "lost explorer" and "unknown" places of Africa were still very much in the minds of English-speaking readers, who hungrily followed the reports of the journalist Henry Morton Stanley on his search for Dr. David Livingstone in the 1870s and Stanley's continued explorations of Africa through the 1890s. Other explorers, such as John Hanning Speke and Sir Richard Francis Burton, also piqued the interest of armchair travelers around the world, and fiction such as the African novels of H. Rider Haggard and Joseph Conrad was widely read. (Though controversial today, Haggard's and Conrad's depictions of Africa and African people were extremely popular with White English and American readers of the day.) At the same time, the activities of Russian spies and the glamour of Russia's extensive nobility were equally appealing. M. P. Shiel's *Prince Zaleski*, published in 1895, was a well-regarded series of mysterious, somewhat supernatural tales of an exiled Russian prince, and works like Leo Tolstoy's *War and Peace* and *Anna Karenina* were reaching widespread English-speaking audiences (both first translated into English in 1886).

Davis's fiction often drew on his own life and experiences. For example, Davis admitted that *The Princess Aline* was drawn from his own infatuation with Princess Alix of Hesse-Darmstadt, who

---

*Dorothy Glover and Graham Greene, *Victorian Detective Fiction: A Catalogue of the Collection* (London: Bodley Head, 1966). The collection was limited to books published before 1900. This editor's collection of pre-1901 crime fiction, which contains only about 130 of the Glover-Greene titles, numbers almost six hundred volumes—that is, more than 450 titles not listed in the Glover-Greene catalogue.

---

†Glover and Greene, viii.

under the name Alexandra Feodorovna served as the czarina of Russia.* The title story in *Gallegher, and Other Stories* was at least partially autobiographical: in 1916, the editor of *The Bookman* stated as fact that there was a real office boy employed by the *Philadelphia Press* named Tommy Gallegher. Davis was assigned by the *Press* to cover a fight in a stable in a Philadelphia suburb, and when the police raided, arresting everyone, Davis slipped his report of the fight to Gallegher, who was able to make his way back to the newspaper offices with the story in time for the morning edition.† However, the crime in "Gallegher," as in the case of *In the Fog*, is fictional.

Davis himself had an adventure in the London fog in 1897, the same year in which he set this tale, which was not unlike the events of the story. He had just finished Christmas dinner at the home of actress Cecilia "Cissie" Loftus and her husband, Justin McCarthy, in the company of their mutual friend, the legendary actress Ethel Barrymore. Davis and Barrymore left the McCarthys' around 11:00 p.m. Here is his own version:

> *There was a light fog. I said that all sorts of things ought to happen in a fog but that no one ever did have adventures nowadays. At that we rode straight into a bank of fog that makes those on the fishing banks look like Spring sunshine. You could not see the houses, nor the street, nor the horse, not even his tail.... The cabman discovered the fact that*

---

*Kenneth Whyte, *The Uncrowned King: The Sensational Rise of William Randolph Hearst* (Berkeley, CA: Counterpoint, 2009), 280.

---

†"Chronicle and Comment," *The Bookman* 43 (June 1916): 356. The column was probably written by G. G. Wynant, who had recently become the editor of the magazine, taking over from the longtime editor Arthur Bartlett Maurice. The story is of questionable veracity. Some *Evening Sun* (New York) reporters believed that "Gallegher" was based on an office boy at the *Sun* named "Daddy" Reaper, who was devoted to Davis. Cited in Arthur Lubow's *The Reporter Who Would Be King: A Biography of Richard Harding Davis* (New York: Charles Scribner's Sons, 1992), 65n92.

he was lost and turned around in circles and the horse
slipped on the asphalt which was thick with frost, and
then we backed into lamp-posts and curbs until Ethel got
so scared she bit her under lip until it bled. You could not
tell whether you were going into a house or over a precipice
or into a sea. The horse finally backed up a flight of steps,
and rubbed the cabby against a front door, and jabbed the
wheels into an area railing and fell down. That, I thought,
was our cue to get out, so we slipped into a well of yellow
mist and felt around for each other until a square block
of light suddenly opened in mid air and four terrified
women appeared in the doorway of the house through
which the cabman was endeavoring to butt himself. They
begged us to come in, and we did—Being Christmas and
because the McCarthys always call me "King" I had put
on all my decorations and the tin star and I also wore my
beautiful fur coat... I took this off because the room was
very hot, forgetting about the decorations and remarked
in the same time to Ethel that it would be folly to try and
get to Barkston Gardens, and that we must go back to the
"Duchess's" for the night. At this Ethel answered calmly,
"yes, Duke," and I became conscious of the fact that the
eyes of the four women were riveted on my fur coat and
decorations. At the word "Duke" delivered by a very pretty
girl in an evening frock and with nothing on her hair the
four women disappeared and brought back the children,
the servants, and the men, who were so overcome with
awe and excitement and Christmas cheer that they all but
got down on their knees in a circle. So, we fled out into
the night followed by minute directions as to where "Your
Grace" and "Your Ladyship" should turn. For years, no
doubt, on a Christmas Day the story will be told in that

*house, wherever it may be in the millions of other houses of London, how a beautiful Countess and a wicked Duke were pitched into their front door out of a hansom cab, and after having partaken of their Christmas supper, disappeared again into a sea of fog.**

Four years later, the imagination of Davis, still only thirty-seven, would spin a series of yarns that took shape from his own respite from the fog. Did Davis imagine himself as the dashing young American lieutenant? Was the Russian beauty another incarnation of his Princess Alix? These questions are intriguing but wholly irrelevant to enjoyment of this brisk tale. And so, into the fog...

—Leslie S. Klinger

---

*Letter to Davis's mother, Rebecca Harding Davis, dated December 29, 1897, published in Charles Belmont Davis, ed., *Adventures and Letters of Richard Harding Davis* (New York: Charles Scribner's Sons, 1917), 220–21.

CHAPTER I

The Grill is the club most difficult of access in the world.* To be placed on its rolls† distinguishes the new member as greatly as though he had received a vacant Garter‡ or had been caricatured in "Vanity Fair."§

---

*In 1897, more than one hundred social clubs flourished in London (with more than forty of them still in existence in 2023). An excellent list can be found in the 1896 *Baedeker's London and Its Environs* (Leipsic: Karl Baedeker), and the colorful history of the clubs is recounted in the excellent *London Clubs: Their History and Treasures* by Ralph Nevill (London: Chatto & Windus, 1911). Some were based on preexisting affiliations—a sporting interest, a university connection, a shared military experience, or a political leaning—but many were purely social. Almost all were exclusively male and offered a sanctuary for upper-class men, as pubs were for the lower classes. Many offered gambling, alcoholic beverages, meals (said to exceed restaurants in quality), and in some cases lodging. "Clubland," in or near Pall Mall, housed the most prominent clubs. Members were admitted by ballot, but candidates could be rejected by a certain small proportion of the members who cast "black balls," dissenting votes.

†That is, to be made a member.

‡There are only twenty-four knights of the Order of the Garter (founded in the fourteenth century by Edward III), the highest order of chivalry in England.

§The popular London magazine *Vanity Fair* (1868–1914), the best of the "society" magazines of the day, published more than 2,800 caricatures of athletes, artists, statesmen, royalty, and literary, theatrical, political, and other popular figures. The National Portrait Gallery, in an exhibition of the caricatures, remarked, "It gradually became a mark of honour to be the 'victim' of one of its numerous caricaturists" (Elizabeth Heath, "Vanity Fair Cartoons: Drawings by Various Artists, 1869–1910," National

Men who belong to the Grill Club never mention that fact. If you were to ask one of them which clubs he frequents, he will name all save that particular one. He is afraid if he told you he belonged to the Grill, that it would sound like boasting.

The Grill Club dates back to the days when Shakespeare's Theatre stood on the present site of the "Times" office.* It has a golden Grill which Charles the Second presented to the Club,† and the original manuscript of "Tom and Jerry in London," which was bequeathed to it by Pierce Egan himself.‡ The members, when they write letters at the Club, still use sand to blot the ink.

The Grill enjoys the distinction of having blackballed, without political prejudice, a Prime Minister of each party. At the same sitting at which one of these fell, it elected, on account of

---

Portrait Gallery, https://www.npg.org.uk/collections/search/set/361/Vanity+Fair+cartoons).

The Times [of London] was produced from 1785 to 1974 at Printing House Square, off Queen Victoria Street. The offices encompassed the refectory of Blackfriar Priory, where Shakespeare staged plays in the winter, when the Globe Theatre was closed. Note that the narrator isn't saying where the Grill Club is, only its antiquity. However, a few sentences later, the narrator suggests that the Club is at least a hundred years older than the *Times* offices.

---

†Charles II died in 1685, so the presentation was in the late seventeenth century. The clubs of that era were really coffeehouses, frequented by persons with common interests. For example, Lloyd's was a coffeehouse whose members were generally insurers, especially of shipping. It is impossible to trace which coffeehouse may have been rechristened as the Grill Club, and there was no actual club with that name in 1897.

---

‡*Life in London; or, The Day and Night Scenes of Jerry Hawthorn, Esq., and His Elegant Friend, Corinthian Tom, Accompanied by Bob Logic, the Oxonian, in Their Rambles and Sprees through the Metropolis* was a very successful book by Pierce Egan, published in 1821 and immediately adapted by Egan into a popular stage play titled *Tom and Jerry, or Life in London*. The characters of Tom and Jerry became synonymous with wild, bohemian behavior, gave their names to a popular Christmas drink, and probably inspired the choice of names for the eponymous cat and mouse cartoon characters created in 1940 by Hanna-Barbera.

his brogue and his bulls,[*] Quiller, Q. C., who was then a penniless barrister.[†]

When Paul Preval,[‡] the French artist who came to London by royal command to paint a portrait of the Prince of Wales, was made an honorary member—only foreigners may be honorary members—he said, as he signed his first wine-card, "I would rather see my name on that, than on a picture in the Louvre."

At which Quiller remarked, "That is a devil of a compliment, because the only men who can read their names in the Louvre to-day have been dead fifty years."[§]

On the night after the great fog of 1897[¶] there were five members in the Club, four of them busy with supper and one reading in front of the fireplace. There is only one room to the Club, and one long table. At the far end of the room the fire of the grill glows red, and, when the fat falls, blazes into flame, and at the other there is

---

*The phrase "brogue and bulls" is meant to convey Quiller as a stereotypical Irishman. A "brogue" is a strongly marked accent, now generally referring to an Irish accent. A "bull" is a traditional form of Irish humor, a wordplay, sometimes intentional, sometimes inadvertent—a malapropism that suggests that the speaker is ignorant of the English language. For example, in George Farquhar's 1704 stage play *The Stage-Coach*, Macahone, a character described as a "booby" but also as an "Irish wit," says that his home is "my Mansionhouse for me and my Predecessors after me."

---

†A "Q. C. " or "K. C. " is an honorific meaning "Queen's [or King's] Counsel," i.e., honored by the monarch as an outstanding advocate, usually a barrister (a trial lawyer).

---

‡A fictional artist.

---

§Probably in part because the creators were living artists, the Louvre did not include the monumental creations of the Impressionists and post-Impressionists in its collection until the 1920s.

¶1897 was a peaceful year for England, marked primarily by the sixtieth anniversary of the accession of Queen Victoria to the throne, her "Diamond Jubilee." Victoria was the first British monarch to enjoy such an anniversary, a record subsequently broken by Elizabeth II, who sat on the throne for seventy years and seven months. The *St. James's Gazette* of December 24, 1897, reported, in an article titled "The City of Dreadful Night," "For the greater part of the week, fog has prevailed in London.... Many people got lost in the fog, and boys with torches were in great requisition to guide wayfarers to their homes" (9).

a broad bow window of diamond panes, which looks down upon the street. The four men at the table were strangers to each other, but as they picked at the grilled bones, and sipped their Scotch and soda, they conversed with such charming animation that a visitor to the Club, which does not tolerate visitors, would have counted them as friends of long acquaintance, certainly not as Englishmen who had met for the first time, and without the form of an introduction.* But it is the etiquette and tradition of the Grill, that whoever enters it must speak with whomever he finds there. It is to enforce this rule that there is but one long table, and whether there are twenty men at it or two, the waiters, supporting the rule, will place them side by side.

For this reason the four strangers at supper were seated together, with the candles grouped about them, and the long length of the table cutting a white path through the outer gloom.

"I repeat," said the gentleman with the black pearl stud, "that the days for romantic adventure and deeds of foolish daring have passed, and that the fault lies with ourselves. Voyages to the pole I do not catalogue as adventures. That African explorer, young Chetney, who turned up yesterday after he was supposed to have died in Uganda,† did nothing adventurous.

*Spoiler alert: Note that Davis is careful to record that the storytellers were "strangers to each other." Therefore, we must understand that the idea of spinning the yarn arose spontaneously in the mind of Lieutenant Sears, and the others merely took up his plan as he spoke. The lieutenant was apparently quite taken with the idea of preventing Sir Andrew from participating in the vote. Did he have ulterior motives? Certainly the American government would not have wished to see its maritime rival Great Britain build more warships.

†Uganda lies in the middle of central Africa and was at this time a protectorate of the British Empire. Earlier, many explorers—including the missionary Dr. David Livingstone—had gone there searching for the source of the Nile River. Livingstone was famously "lost," out of contact with the Western world for six years. In 1869, Henry Morton Stanley, a newspaper reporter, traveled to Africa to find Livingstone, eventually meeting him in 1871. The popularity of the story was so great that novelists such as H. Rider Haggard and Joseph Conrad wrote their own powerful tales of African explorations.

"The four strangers at supper were seated together."

He made maps and explored the sources of rivers. He was in constant danger, but the presence of danger does not constitute adventure. Were that so, the chemist who studies high explosives, or who investigates deadly poisons, passes through adventures daily. No, 'adventures are for the adventurous.' But one no longer ventures. The spirit of it has died of inertia. We are grown too practical, too just, above all, too sensible. In this room, for instance, members of this Club have, at the sword's point, disputed the proper scanning of one of Pope's couplets.* Over so weighty a matter as spilled Burgundy on a gentleman's cuff, ten men fought across this table, each with his rapier in one hand and a candle in the other. All ten were wounded. The question of the spilled Burgundy concerned but two of them. The eight others engaged because they were men of 'spirit.' They were, indeed, the first gentlemen of the day. To-night, were you to spill Burgundy on my cuff, were you even to insult me grossly, these gentlemen would not consider it incumbent upon them to kill each other. They would separate us, and to-morrow morning appear as witnesses against us at Bow Street.† We have here to-

---

*Alexander Pope (1688–1744), that is, one of England's greatest poets.

---

†The police court.

night, in the persons of Sir Andrew* and myself, an illustration of how the ways have changed."

"The men around the table turned and glanced
toward the gentleman in front of the fireplace."

The men around the table turned and glanced toward the gentleman in front of the fireplace. He was an elderly and somewhat portly person, with a kindly, wrinkled countenance, which wore continually a smile of almost childish confidence and good-nature. It was a face which the illustrated prints had made

---

*Sir Andrew, we will learn, is a baronet—the lowest level of hereditary title, often conferred for achievements or contributions, and not a member of the peerage. A baronet might be styled "Sir Andrew Richardson, Bt. [or Bart.]" or familiarly called "Sir Andrew" (never "Sir Richardson"). His children bear no titles. Baronets are not titled peers who sit in the House of Lords (the lowest rank there is a baron); however, as we will see, Sir Andrew is a member of Parliament, who must therefore sit in the House of Commons, an elected branch of the British government.

intimately familiar. He held a book from him at arm's-length, as if to adjust his eyesight, and his brows were knit with interest.

"Now, were this the eighteenth century," continued the gentleman with the black pearl, "when Sir Andrew left the Club to-night I would have him bound and gagged and thrown into a sedan chair. The watch would not interfere, the passers-by would take to their heels, my hired bullies and ruffians would convey him to some lonely spot where we would guard him until morning. Nothing would come of it, except added reputation to myself as a gentleman of adventurous spirit, and possibly an essay in the 'Tatler,'* with stars for names, entitled, let us say, 'The Budget and the Baronet.'"

"But to what end, sir?" inquired the youngest of the members. "And why Sir Andrew, of all persons—why should you select him for this adventure?"

The gentleman with the black pearl shrugged his shoulders.

"It would prevent him speaking in the House to-night. The Navy Increase Bill,"† he added gloomily. "It is a Government measure, and Sir Andrew speaks for it. And so great is his influence and so large his following that if he does"—the gentleman laughed ruefully—"if he does, it will go through. Now, had I the spirit of our ancestors," he exclaimed, "I would bring chloroform from the nearest chemist's and drug him in that chair. I would tumble his unconscious form into a hansom cab, and hold him prisoner until daylight. If I did, I would save the British taxpayer the cost of five more battleships, many millions of pounds."

---

*The Tatler was a gossip magazine published between 1709 and 1711, with a style mixing real and fictional stories about life in London that was later copied by *The Spectator*, Samuel Johnson's *Rambler* and *Idler*, and Oliver Goldsmith's *Citizen of the World*.

---

†The Navy Increase Bill is a budgetary bill allotting funds to the British Admiralty. The British Naval Works Bill of 1897 added appropriations for docks and harbors; the admiralty pointed out that previous budgets had already increased the number of ships, and under those budgets seventy-one additional ships would come online by the end of the 1897–98 fiscal year. The bill passed on July 29 after a second reading.

"I would tumble his unconscious form into a hansom
cab, and hold him prisoner until daylight."

The gentlemen again turned, and surveyed the Baronet
with freshened interest. The honorary member of the Grill,
whose accent already had betrayed him as an American,
laughed softly.

"To look at him now," he said, "one would not guess he was
deeply concerned with the affairs of state."

The others nodded silently.

"He has not lifted his eyes from that book since we first entered," added the youngest member. "He surely cannot mean to speak to-night."

"Oh, yes, he will speak," muttered the one with the black pearl moodily. "During these last hours of the session the House sits late, but when the Navy bill comes up on its third reading he will be in his place—and he will pass it."

The fourth member, a stout and florid gentleman of a somewhat sporting appearance, in a short smoking-jacket and black tie, sighed enviously.

"Fancy one of us being as cool as that, if he knew he had to stand up within an hour and rattle off a speech in Parliament. I'd be in a devil of a funk myself. And yet he is as keen over that book he's reading as though he had nothing before him until bedtime."

"Yes, see how eager he is," whispered the youngest member. "He does not lift his eyes even now when he cuts the pages. It is probably an Admiralty Report, or some other weighty work of statistics which bears upon his speech."

The gentleman with the black pearl laughed morosely.

"The weighty work in which the eminent statesman is so deeply engrossed," he said, "is called 'The Great Rand Robbery.'* It is a detective novel, for sale at all bookstalls."

The American raised his eyebrows in disbelief.

"'The Great Rand Robbery'?" he repeated incredulously. "What an odd taste!"

"It is not a taste, it is his vice," returned the gentleman with the pearl stud. "It is his one dissipation. He is noted for it. You,

---

*Although detective novels were indeed the rage, this is a fictitious title, inspired by Julian Hawthorne's 1887 novel *The Great Bank Robbery* or, more likely, the popular stage play *The Great Diamond Robbery*, by Edmund M. Alfriend and A. C. Wheeler, which opened on Broadway in 1895 and was made into a silent film in 1914. The Rand (short for the Witwatersrand) was the prolific gold-mining region in what is now the Gauteng province of South Africa.

as a stranger, could hardly be expected to know of this idiosyncrasy. Mr. Gladstone sought relaxation in the Greek poets,[*] Sir Andrew finds his in Gaboriau.[†] Since I have been a member of Parliament I have never seen him in the library without a shilling shocker in his hands. He brings them even into the sacred precincts of the House, and from the Government benches[‡] reads them concealed inside his hat. Once started on a tale of murder, robbery, and sudden death, nothing can tear him from it, not even the call of the division bell, nor of hunger, nor the prayers of the party Whip. He gave up his country house because when he journeyed to it in the train he would become so absorbed in his detective stories that he was invariably carried past his station." The member of Parliament twisted his pearl stud nervously, and bit at the edge of his mustache. "If it only were the first pages of 'The Rand Robbery' that he were reading," he murmured bitterly, "instead of the last! With such another book as that, I swear I could hold him here until morning. There would be no need of chloroform to keep him from the House."

The eyes of all were fastened upon Sir Andrew, and each saw with fascination that with his forefinger he was now separating the last two pages of the book. The member of Parliament struck the table softly with his open palm.

"I would give a hundred pounds," he whispered, "if I could place in his hands at this moment a new story of Sherlock Holmes—a thousand pounds," he added wildly—"five thousand pounds!"[§]

---

[*]Indeed, William Gladstone wrote a book on them: *Studies on Homer and the Homeric Age*, published in 1858, ten years before he first became prime minister.

[†]See note in the introduction, page xii.

[‡]That is, the seats where the members of the ruling party would be seated. In 1897, the House of Commons was dominated by the Conservatives and the Liberal Unionists, who had come into power in the 1895 general election, and Robert Gascoyne-Cecil, Marquess of Salisbury, was the prime minister.

[§]Alas for the speaker, in 1897, Sherlock Holmes was missing from the pages of the

The American observed the speaker sharply, as though the words bore to him some special application, and then at an idea which apparently had but just come to him, smiled in great embarrassment.

Sir Andrew ceased reading, but, as though still under the influence of the book, sat looking blankly into the open fire. For a brief space no one moved until the Baronet withdrew his eyes and, with a sudden start of recollection, felt anxiously for his watch. He scanned its face eagerly, and scrambled to his feet.

The voice of the American instantly broke the silence in a high, nervous accent.

"And yet Sherlock Holmes himself," he cried, "could not decipher the mystery which to-night baffles the police of London."

At these unexpected words, which carried in them something of the tone of a challenge, the gentlemen about the table started as suddenly as though the American had fired a pistol in the air, and Sir Andrew halted abruptly and stood observing him with grave surprise.

The gentleman with the black pearl was the first to recover.

"Yes, yes," he said eagerly, throwing himself across the table. "A mystery that baffles the police of London. I have heard nothing of it. Tell us at once, pray do—tell us at once."

The American flushed uncomfortably, and picked uneasily at the tablecloth.

"No one but the police has heard of it," he murmured, "and they only through me. It is a remarkable crime, to which, unfortunately, I am the only person who can bear witness. Because I

Strand Magazine, presumed dead by its readers. The last story before 1897, "The Final Problem," appeared in the December 1893 issue, and in it, Sherlock Holmes vanished over the Reichenbach Falls in the clutches of the "Napoleon of crime," Professor Moriarty. Although neither the speaker nor Davis knew this, in fact, no new tale of Holmes would appear until August 1901, when *The Hound of the Baskervilles* began to appear in serial form in the *Strand Magazine*.

am the only witness, I am, in spite of my immunity as a diplomat, detained in London by the authorities of Scotland Yard. My name," he said, inclining his head politely, "is Sears, Lieutenant Ripley Sears of the United States Navy, at present Naval Attaché to the Court of Russia.* Had I not been detained to-day by the police I would have started this morning for Petersburg."

"My name," he said, "is Sears."

---

*The relationship between the United States and Russia was generally positive at this point, as was the relationship between the United Kingdom and Russia. They had common interests in suppressing the Boxer Rebellion, protecting their interests in China, and promoting expansion of commerce in the Far East. The United States was grateful to Russia for its support of the Union during the Civil War, but the czar suffered a poor reputation among Americans, especially for his anti-Jewish pogroms. England had a longer and more turbulent history with Russia. The two nations had long sparred in India, in a series of intrigues known as the "Great Game," and so it was to be expected that each nation would spy on the other. By 1897, however, matters had cooled. The czar, Nicholas II, was related to Queen Victoria through his wife, the queen's granddaughter Alexandra (previously known as Princess Alix of Hesse), and enjoyed a warm friendship, culminating in his state visit to Balmoral Castle in 1896.

The gentleman with the black pearl interrupted with so pronounced an exclamation of excitement and delight that the American stammered and ceased speaking.

"Do you hear, Sir Andrew?" cried the member of Parliament jubilantly. "An American diplomat halted by our police because he is the only witness of a most remarkable crime—*the* most remarkable crime, I believe you said, sir," he added, bending eagerly toward the naval officer, "which has occurred in London in many years."

The American moved his head in assent and glanced at the two other members. They were looking doubtfully at him, and the face of each showed that he was greatly perplexed.

Sir Andrew advanced to within the light of the candles and drew a chair toward him.

"The crime must be exceptional indeed," he said, "to justify the police in interfering with a representative of a friendly power. If I were not forced to leave at once, I should take the liberty of asking you to tell us the details."

The gentleman with the pearl pushed the chair toward Sir Andrew, and motioned him to be seated.

"You cannot leave us now," he exclaimed. "Mr. Sears is just about to tell us of this remarkable crime."

He nodded vigorously at the naval officer and the American, after first glancing doubtfully toward the servants at the far end of the room, leaned forward across the table. The others drew their chairs nearer and bent toward him. The Baronet glanced irresolutely at his watch, and with an exclamation of annoyance snapped down the lid. "They can wait," he muttered. He seated himself quickly and nodded at Lieutenant Sears.

"If you will be so kind as to begin, sir," he said impatiently.

"Of course," said the American, "you understand that I understand that I am speaking to gentlemen. The confidences of this Club are inviolate. Until the police give the facts to the public press, I must consider you my confederates. You have heard nothing, you know no one connected with this mystery. Even I must remain anonymous."

The gentlemen seated around him nodded gravely.

"Of course," the Baronet assented with eagerness, "of course."

"We will refer to it," said the gentleman with the black pearl, "as 'The Story of the Naval Attaché.'"

"I arrived in London two days ago," said the American, "and I engaged a room at the Bath Hotel.* I know very few people in London, and even the members of our embassy were strangers to me. But in Hong Kong I had become great pals with an officer in your navy, who has since retired, and who is now living in a small house in Rutland Gardens opposite the Knightsbridge Barracks.† I telegraphed him that I was in London, and yesterday morning I received a most hearty invitation to dine with him the same evening at his house. He is a bachelor, so we dined alone and talked over all our old days on the Asiatic Station, and of the changes which had come to us since we had last met there. As I was leaving the next morning for my post at Petersburg, and had many letters to write, I told him, about ten o'clock, that I must get back to the hotel, and he sent out his servant to call a hansom.

"For the next quarter of an hour, as we sat talking, we could hear the cab whistle sounding violently from the doorstep, but apparently with no result.

"'It cannot be that the cabmen are on strike,' my friend said, as he rose and walked to the window.

"He pulled back the curtains and at once called to me.

---

*A hotel at the corner of Arlington Street, on the south side of Piccadilly, noted in *Baedeker's London and Its Environs* (1896).

---

†The Hyde Park Barracks, known locally as the Knightsbridge Barracks, were substantially expanded in 1880. Located about three-quarters of a mile from Buckingham Palace, they house the Household Cavalry.

'"You have never seen a London fog, have you?' he asked. 'Well, come here. This is one of the best, or, rather, one of the worst, of them.' I joined him at the window, but I could see nothing. Had I not known that the house looked out upon the street I would have believed that I was facing a dead wall. I raised the sash and stretched out my head, but still I could see nothing. Even the light of the street lamps opposite, and in the upper windows of the barracks, had been smothered in the yellow mist.* The lights of the room in which I stood penetrated the fog only to the distance of a few inches from my eyes.

"Below me the servant was still sounding his whistle, but I could afford to wait no longer, and told my friend that I would try and find the way to my hotel on foot. He objected, but the letters I had to write were for the Navy Department, and, besides, I had always heard that to be out in a London fog was the most wonderful experience, and I was curious to investigate one for myself.

"My friend went with me to his front door, and laid down a course for me to follow. I was first to walk straight across the street to the brick wall of the Knightsbridge Barracks. I was then to feel my way along the wall until I came to a row of houses set back from the sidewalk. They would bring me to a cross street. On the other side of this street was a row of shops which I was to follow until they joined the iron railings of Hyde Park. I was to keep to the railings until I reached the gates at Hyde Park Corner, where I was to lay a diagonal course across Piccadilly, and tack in toward the railings of Green Park. At the end of these railings, going east, I would find the Walsingham,† and my own hotel.

---

*It should be remembered that until the 1930s, fully half of the streets of London were still lit by gas lamps.

---

†The Walsingham House Hotel was almost directly adjacent to the Bath Hotel, at 150–54 Piccadilly, on what is now the site of the Ritz Hotel. Curiously, it is not mentioned

"To a sailor the course did not seem difficult, so I bade my friend goodnight and walked forward until my feet touched the paving. I continued upon it until I reached the curbing of the sidewalk. A few steps further, and my hands struck the wall of the barracks. I turned in the direction from which I had just come, and saw a square of faint light cut in the yellow fog. I shouted 'All right,' and the voice of my friend answered, 'Good luck to you.' The light from his open door disappeared with a bang, and I was left alone in a dripping, yellow darkness. I have been in the Navy for ten years, but I have never known such a fog as that of last night, not even among the icebergs of Behring Sea.* There one at least could see the light of the binnacle,† but last night I could not even distinguish the hand by which I guided myself along the barrack wall. At sea a fog is a natural phenomenon. It is as familiar as the rainbow which follows a storm, it is as proper that a fog should spread upon the waters as that steam shall rise from a kettle. But a fog which springs from the paved streets, that rolls between solid house-fronts, that forces cabs to move at half speed, that drowns policemen and extinguishes the electric lights of the music hall, that to me is incomprehensible. It is as out of place as a tidal wave on Broadway.

"As I felt my way along the wall, I encountered other men who were coming from the opposite direction, and each time when we hailed each other I stepped away from the wall to make room for them to pass. But the third time I did this, when I reached out my hand, the wall had disappeared, and the further

in the 1896 Baedeker guide, possibly because it featured large six-bedroom flats and catered more to long-term tenants.

---

*Usually spelled Bering, and named after the Danish navigator Vitus Jonassen Bering, this is the far northern body of water separating the landmass of Eurasia from North America. The Navy did patrol these cold and foggy waters, which were sailed heavily by seal hunters.

---

†The housing for the ship's compass, usually including an oil lamp by which to read the compass.

I moved to find it the further I seemed to be sinking into space. I had the unpleasant conviction that at any moment I might step over a precipice. Since I had set out I had heard no traffic in the street, and now, although I listened some minutes, I could only distinguish the occasional footfalls of pedestrians. Several times I called aloud, and once a jocular gentleman answered me, but only to ask me where I thought he was, and then even he was swallowed up in the silence. Just above me I could make out a jet of gas which I guessed came from a street lamp, and I moved over to that, and, while I tried to recover my bearings, kept my hand on the iron post. Except for this flicker of gas, no larger than the tip of my finger, I could distinguish nothing about me. For the rest, the mist hung between me and the world like a damp and heavy blanket.

"A square of light suddenly opened in the night and in it I saw a young gentleman in evening dress."

"I could hear voices, but I could not tell from whence they came, and the scrape of a foot moving cautiously, or a muffled cry as some one stumbled, were the only sounds that reached me.

"I decided that until some one took me in tow I had best remain where I was, and it must have been for ten minutes that I waited by the lamp, straining my ears and hailing distant footfalls. In a house near me some people were dancing to the music of a Hungarian band. I even fancied I could hear the windows shake to the rhythm of their feet, but I could not make out from which part of the compass the sounds came. And sometimes, as the music rose, it seemed close at my hand, and again, to be floating high in the air above my head. Although I was surrounded by thousands of householders, I was as completely lost as though I had been set down by night in the Sahara Desert. There seemed to be no reason in waiting longer for an escort, so I again set out, and at once bumped against a low iron fence. At first I believed this to be an area railing, but on following it I found that it stretched for a long distance, and that it was pierced at regular intervals with gates. I was standing uncertainly with my hand on one of these when a square of light suddenly opened in the night, and in it I saw, as you see a picture thrown by a biograph* in a darkened theatre, a young gentleman in evening dress, and back of him the lights of a hall. I guessed from its elevation and distance from the sidewalk that this light must come from the door of a house set back from the street, and I determined to approach it and ask the young man to tell me where I was. But in fumbling with the lock of the gate I instinctively bent my head, and when I raised it again the door had partly closed, leaving only a narrow shaft of light. Whether the young

---

*An early form of movie projector. The American Mutoscope Company, one of the earliest American film companies, became the American Mutoscope and Biograph Company in 1899, and the Biograph Company in 1909.

man had re-entered the house, or had left it I could not tell, but I hastened to open the gate, and as I stepped forward I found myself upon an asphalt walk. At the same instant there was the sound of quick steps upon the path, and some one rushed past me. I called to him, but he made no reply, and I heard the gate click and the footsteps hurrying away upon the sidewalk.

"Under other circumstances the young man's rudeness, and his recklessness in dashing so hurriedly through the mist, would have struck me as peculiar, but everything was so distorted by the fog that at the moment I did not consider it. The door was still as he had left it, partly open. I went up the path, and, after much fumbling, found the knob of the door-bell and gave it a sharp pull. The bell answered me from a great depth and distance, but no movement followed from inside the house, and although I pulled the bell again and again I could hear nothing save the dripping of the mist about me. I was anxious to be on my way, but unless I knew where I was going there was little chance of my making any speed, and I was determined that until I learned my bearings I would not venture back into the fog. So I pushed the door open and stepped into the house.

"I found myself in a long and narrow hall, upon which doors opened from either side. At the end of the hall was a staircase with a balustrade which ended in a sweeping curve. The balustrade was covered with heavy Persian rugs, and the walls of the hall were also hung with them. The door on my left was closed, but the one nearer me on the right was open, and as I stepped opposite to it I saw that it was a sort of reception or waiting-room, and that it was empty. The door below it was also open, and with the idea that I would surely find some one there, I walked on up the hall. I was in evening dress, and I felt I did not look like a burglar, so I had no great fear that, should I encounter one of the inmates of the house, he would shoot me on sight.

The second door in the hall opened into a dining-room. This was also empty. One person had been dining at the table, but the cloth had not been cleared away, and a nickering candle showed half-filled wineglasses and the ashes of cigarettes. The greater part of the room was in complete darkness.

"By this time I had grown conscious of the fact that I was wandering about in a strange house, and that, apparently, I was alone in it. The silence of the place began to try my nerves, and in a sudden, unexplainable panic I started for the open street. But as I turned, I saw a man sitting on a bench, which the curve of the balustrade had hidden from me. His eyes were shut, and he was sleeping soundly.

"The moment before I had been bewildered because I could see no one, but at sight of this man I was much more bewildered.

"He was a very large man, a giant in height, with long yellow hair which hung below his shoulders. He was dressed in a red silk shirt that was belted at the waist and hung outside black velvet trousers which, in turn, were stuffed into high black boots. I recognized the costume at once as that of a Russian servant, but what a Russian servant in his native livery could be doing in a private house in Knightsbridge was incomprehensible.*

"I advanced and touched the man on the shoulder, and after an effort he awoke, and, on seeing me, sprang to his feet and began bowing rapidly and making deprecatory gestures. I had picked up enough Russian in Petersburg to make out that the

---

*By this date, Americans had developed a deep sympathy for the Russian peasants, and the regime of the czar and its treatment of the peasantry were widely criticized in the United States. It wasn't until the abdication of the czar in 1917 that Americans could wholeheartedly ally with Russia in World War I against Germany and its allies. Nonetheless, this must be viewed as a rather caricatured portrayal of a Russian peasant—dressed in "native livery," subservient, and indulgent in heavy drink on a religious holiday.

man was apologizing for having fallen asleep, and I also was able to explain to him, that I desired to see his master.

"He nodded vigorously, and said, 'Will the Excellency come this way? The Princess is here.'

"I distinctly made out the word 'princess,' and I was a good deal embarrassed. I had thought it would be easy enough to explain my intrusion to a man, but how a woman would look at it was another matter, and as I followed him down the hall I was somewhat puzzled.

"As we advanced, he noticed that the front door was standing open, and with an exclamation of surprise, hastened toward it and closed it. Then he rapped twice on the door of what was apparently the drawing-room. There was no reply to his knock, and he tapped again, and then timidly, and cringing subserviently, opened the door and stepped inside. He withdrew himself at once and stared stupidly at me, shaking his head.

"'She is not there,' he said. He stood for a moment gazing blankly through the open door, and then hastened toward the dining-room. The solitary candle which still burned there seemed to assure him that the room also was empty. He came back and bowed me toward the drawing-room. 'She is above,' he said; 'I will inform the Princess of the Excellency's presence.'

"Before I could stop him he had turned and was running up the staircase, leaving me alone at the open door of the drawing-room. I decided that the adventure had gone quite far enough, and if I had been able to explain to the Russian that I had lost my way in the fog, and only wanted to get back into the street again, I would have left the house on the instant.

"Of course, when I first rang the bell of the house I had no other expectation than that it would be answered by a parlormaid who would direct me on my way. I certainly could not then foresee that I would disturb a Russian princess* in her boudoir, or that I might be thrown out by her athletic bodyguard. Still, I thought I ought not now to leave the house without making some apology, and, if the worst should come, I could show my card. They could hardly believe that a member of an embassy had any designs upon the hat-rack.

"The room in which I stood was dimly lighted, but I could see that, like the hall, it was hung with heavy Persian rugs. The corners were filled with palms, and there was the unmistakable odor in the air of Russian cigarettes,† and strange, dry scents that carried me back to the bazaars of Vladivostock. Near the front windows was a grand piano, and at the other end of the room a heavily carved screen of some black wood, picked out with ivory. The screen was overhung with a canopy of silken draperies, and formed a sort of alcove. In front of the alcove was spread the white skin of a polar bear, and set on that was one of those low Turkish coffee tables. It held a lighted spirit-lamp and two gold coffee cups. I had heard no movement from above stairs, and it must have been fully three minutes that I stood waiting, noting these details of the room and wondering at the delay, and at the strange silence.

"And then, suddenly, as my eye grew more used to the half-light, I saw, projecting from behind the screen as though it were stretched along the back of a divan, the hand of a man and the lower part of his arm. I was as startled as though I had come across a footprint on a deserted island. Evidently the man had

---

*Richard Harding Davis was said to be infatuated with Alexandra Feodorovna, the consort of Czar Nicholas II, who clearly inspired the character of Princess Aline in Davis's popular eponymous 1895 novella.

†In 1897, *papirosy*, which used a hollow, cardboard tube mouthpiece affixed to tissue paper–wrapped "cartridges" of tobacco, dominated the Russian tobacco market; pipes and cigars were uncommon. *Papirosy* generally used strong-smelling, rough-tasting tobacco, very different from the milder, sweeter Western tobacco.

been sitting there since I had come into the room, even since I had entered the house, and he had heard the servant knocking upon the door. Why he had not declared himself I could not understand, but I supposed that possibly he was a guest, with no reason to interest himself in the Princess's other visitors, or perhaps, for some reason, he did not wish to be observed. I could see nothing of him except his hand, but I had an unpleasant feeling that he had been peering at me through the carving in the screen, and that he still was doing so. I moved my feet noisily on the floor and said tentatively, 'I beg your pardon.'

"There was no reply, and the hand did not stir. Apparently the man was bent upon ignoring me, but as all I wished was to apologize for my intrusion and to leave the house, I walked up to the alcove and peered around it. Inside the screen was a divan piled with cushions, and on the end of it nearer me the man was sitting. He was a young Englishman with light yellow hair and a deeply bronzed face. He was seated with his arms stretched out along the back of the divan, and with his head resting against a cushion. His attitude was one of complete ease. But his mouth had fallen open, and his eyes were set with an expression of utter horror. At the first glance I saw that he was quite dead.

"For a flash of time I was too startled to act, but in the same flash I was convinced that the man had met his death from no accident, that he had not died through any ordinary failure of the laws of nature. The expression on his face was much too terrible to be misinterpreted. It spoke as eloquently as words. It told me that before the end had come he had watched his death approach and threaten him.

"I was so sure he had been murdered that I instinctively looked on the floor for the weapon, and, at the same moment, out of concern for my own safety, quickly behind me; but the silence of the house continued unbroken.

"I have seen a great number of dead men; I was on the Asiatic Station during the Japanese-Chinese war.* I was in Port Arthur after the massacre.† So a dead man, for the single reason that he is dead, does not repel me, and, though I knew that there was no hope that this man was alive, still for decency's sake, I felt his pulse, and while I kept my ears alert for any sound from the floors above me, I pulled open his shirt and placed my hand upon his heart. My fingers instantly touched upon the opening of a wound, and as I withdrew them I found them wet with blood. He was in evening dress, and in the wide bosom of his shirt I found a narrow slit, so narrow that in the dim light it was scarcely discernable. The wound was no wider than the smallest blade of a pocket-knife, but when I stripped the shirt away from the chest and left it bare, I found that the weapon, narrow as it was, had been long enough to reach his heart.‡ There is no need to tell you how I felt as I stood by the body of this boy, for he was hardly older than a boy, or of the thoughts that came into my head. I was bitterly sorry for this stranger, bitterly indignant at his murderer, and, at the same time, selfishly concerned for my own safety and for the notoriety which I saw was sure to follow. My instinct was to leave the body where it lay, and to hide myself in the fog, but

---

*China and Japan fought over influence in Korea between July 1894 and April 1895. After a number of defeats, China entered into a treaty in 1895, ceding certain islands to Japan and promising the independence of Korea.

---

†In November 1894, Japanese forces took the city of Lüshunkou, Manchuria (known as Port Arthur). The troops reportedly massacred thousands of civilians. Initially disbelieved by Westerners who thought the Japanese incapable of such atrocities, subsequent investigation confirmed the slaughter. A Japanese soldier recorded in his diary, "As we entered the town of Port Arthur, we saw the head of a Japanese soldier displayed on a wooden stake. This filled us with rage and a desire to crush any Chinese soldier. Anyone we saw in the town, we killed. The streets were filled with corpses, so many they blocked our way." Quoted in Stuart Lone, *Japan's First Modern War: Army and Society in the Conflict with China, 1894–1895* (New York: St. Martin's Press, 1994), 155.

---

‡One would have expected that a stab wound in the chest would bleed copiously, staining the dress shirt bright red.

I also felt that since a succession of accidents had made me the only witness to a crime, my duty was to make myself a good witness and to assist to establish the facts of this murder.

"That it might possibly be a suicide, and not a murder, did not disturb me for a moment. The fact that the weapon had disappeared, and the expression on the boy's face were enough to convince, at least me, that he had had no hand in his own death. I judged it, therefore, of the first importance to discover who was in the house, or, if they had escaped from it, who had been in the house before I entered it. I had seen one man leave it; but all I could tell of him was that he was a young man, that he was in evening dress, and that he had fled in such haste that he had not stopped to close the door behind him.

"The Russian servant I had found apparently asleep, and, unless he acted a part with supreme skill, he was a stupid and ignorant boor, and as innocent of the murder as myself. There was still the Russian princess whom he had expected to find, or had pretended to expect to find, in the same room with the murdered man. I judged that she must now be either upstairs with the servant, or that she had, without his knowledge, already fled from the house. When I recalled his apparently genuine surprise at not finding her in the drawing-room, this latter supposition seemed the more probable. Nevertheless, I decided that it was my duty to make a search, and after a second hurried look for the weapon among the cushions of the divan, and upon the floor, I cautiously crossed the hall and entered the dining-room.

"The single candle was still flickering in the draught, and showed only the white cloth. The rest of the room was draped in shadows. I picked up the candle, and, lifting it high above my head, moved around the corner of the table. Either my nerves were on such a stretch that no shock could strain them further, or my mind was inoculated to horrors, for I did not cry out at what I saw nor retreat from it. Immediately at my feet was the body of a beautiful woman, lying at full length upon the floor, her arms flung out on either side of her, and her white face and shoulders gleaming dully in the unsteady light of the candle. Around her throat was a great chain of diamonds, and the light played upon these and made them flash and blaze in tiny flames. But the woman who wore them was dead, and I was so certain as to how she had died that without an instant's hesitation I dropped on my knees beside her and placed my hands above her heart. My fingers again touched the thin slit of a wound. I had no doubt in my mind but that this was the Russian princess, and when I lowered the candle to her face I was assured that this was so. Her features showed the finest lines of both the Slav and the Jewess; the eyes were black, the hair blue-black and wonderfully heavy, and her skin, even in death, was rich in color. She was a surpassingly beautiful woman.

"I rose and tried to light another candle with the one I held, but I found that my hand was so unsteady that I could not keep the wicks together. It was my intention to again search for this strange dagger which had been used to kill both the English boy and the beautiful princess, but before I could light the second candle I heard footsteps descending the stairs, and the Russian servant appeared in the doorway.

"My face was in darkness, or I am sure that at the sight of it he would have taken alarm, for at that moment I was not sure but that this man himself was the murderer. His own face was plainly visible to me in the light from the hall, and I could see that it wore an expression of dull bewilderment. I stepped quickly toward him and took a firm hold upon his wrist.

"'She is not there,' he said. 'The Princess has gone. They have all gone.'

"'Who have gone?' I demanded. 'Who else has been here?'

"'The two Englishmen,' he said.

"'What two Englishmen?' I demanded. 'What are their names?'

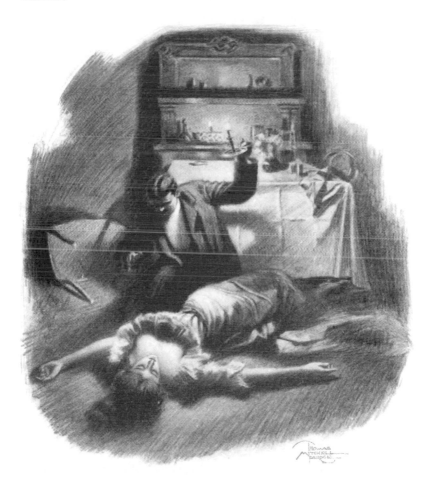

"At my feet was the body of a beautiful woman
lying at full length on the floor."

"The man now saw by my manner that some question of great moment hung upon his answer, and he began to protest that he did not know the names of the visitors and that until that evening he had never seen them.

"I guessed that it was my tone which frightened him, so I took my hand off his wrist and spoke less eagerly.

"'How long have they been here?' I asked, 'and when did they go?'

"He pointed behind him toward the drawing-room.

"'One sat there with the Princess,' he said; 'the other came after I had placed the coffee in the drawing-room. The two Englishmen talked together and the Princess returned here to the table. She sat there in that chair, and I brought her cognac and cigarettes. Then I sat outside upon the bench. It was a feast day,* and I had been drinking. Pardon, Excellency, but I fell asleep. When I woke, your Excellency was standing by me, but the Princess and the two Englishmen had gone. That is all I know.'

"I believed that the man was telling me the truth. His fright had passed, and he was now apparently puzzled, but not alarmed.

"'You must remember the names of the Englishmen,' I urged. 'Try to think. When you announced them to the Princess what name did you give?'

"At this question he exclaimed with pleasure, and, beckoning to me, ran hurriedly down the hall and into the drawing-room. In the corner furthest from the screen was the piano, and on it was a silver tray. He picked this up and, smiling with pride at his own intelligence, pointed at two cards that lay upon it. I took them up and read the names engraved upon them."

The American paused abruptly, and glanced at the faces about him. "I read the names," he repeated. He spoke with great reluctance.

"Continue!" cried the Baronet, sharply.

"I read the names," said the American with evident distaste, "and the family name of each was the same. They were the names of two brothers. One is well known to you. It is that of

---

*That is, the commemoration of a saint in the Russian Orthodox Church.

the African explorer of whom this gentleman was just speaking. I mean the Earl of Chetney. The other was the name of his brother, Lord Arthur Chetney."

The men at the table fell back as though a trapdoor had fallen open at their feet.

"Lord Chetney?" they exclaimed in chorus. They glanced at each other and back to the American with every expression of concern and disbelief.

"It is impossible!" cried the Baronet. "Why, my dear sir, young Chetney only arrived from Africa yesterday. It was so stated in the evening papers."

The jaw of the American set in a resolute square, and he pressed his lips together.

"You are perfectly right, sir," he said, "Lord Chetney did arrive in London yesterday morning, and yesterday night I found his dead body."

The youngest member present was the first to recover. He seemed much less concerned over the identity of the murdered man than at the interruption of the narrative.

"Oh, please let him go on!" he cried. "What happened then? You say you found two visiting cards. How do you know which card was that of the murdered man?"

The American, before he answered, waited until the chorus of exclamations had ceased. Then he continued as though he had not been interrupted.

"The instant I read the names upon the cards," he said, "I ran to the screen and, kneeling beside the dead man, began a search through his pockets. My hand at once fell upon a card-case, and I found on all the cards it contained the title of the Earl of Chetney. His watch and cigarette-case also bore his name. These evidences, and the fact of his bronzed skin, and that his cheekbones were worn with fever, convinced me that the dead man was the African explorer, and the boy who had fled past me in the night was Arthur, his younger brother.

"I was so intent upon my search that I had forgotten the servant, and I was still on my knees when I heard a cry behind me. I turned, and saw the man gazing down at the body in abject horror.

"Before I could rise, he gave another cry of terror, and, flinging himself into the hall, raced toward the door to the street. I leaped after him, shouting to him to halt, but before I could reach the hall he had torn open the door, and I saw him spring out into the yellow fog. I cleared the steps in a jump and ran down the garden walk but just as the gate clicked in front of me. I had it open on the instant, and, following the sound of the man's footsteps, I raced after him across the open street. He, also, could hear me, and he instantly stopped running, and there was absolute silence. He was so near that I almost fancied I could hear him panting, and I held my own breath to listen. But I could distinguish nothing but the dripping of the mist about us, and from far off the music of the Hungarian band, which I had heard when I first lost myself.

"All I could see was the square of light from the door I had left open behind me, and a lamp in the hall beyond it flickering in the draught. But even as I watched it, the flame of the lamp was blown violently to and fro, and the door, caught in the same current of air, closed slowly. I knew if it shut I could not again enter the house, and I rushed madly toward it. I believe I even shouted out, as though it were something human which I could compel to obey me, and then I caught my foot against the curb and smashed into the sidewalk. When I rose to my feet I was dizzy and half stunned, and though I thought then that I was moving toward the door, I know now that I probably turned directly from it; for, as I groped about in the night, calling frantically for the police, my fingers touched nothing but the dripping fog, and the iron railings for which I sought seemed to have melted away. For many minutes I beat the mist with my arms like one at blind man's buff, turning sharply in circles, cursing aloud at my stupidity and crying continually for help. At last a voice answered me from the fog, and I found myself held in the circle of a policeman's lantern.

"That is the end of my adventure. What I have to tell you now is what I learned from the police.

"At the station-house to which the man guided me I related what you have just heard. I told them that the house they must at once find was one set back from the street within a radius of two hundred yards from the Knightsbridge Barracks, that within fifty yards of it some one was giving a dance to the music of a Hungarian band, and that the railings before it were as high as a man's waist and filed to a point. With that to work upon, twenty men were at once ordered out into the fog to search for the house, and Inspector Lyle himself was despatched to the home of Lord Edam, Chetney's father,* with a warrant for Lord Arthur's arrest. I was thanked and dismissed on my own recognizance.

"This morning, Inspector Lyle called on me, and from him I learned the police theory of the scene I have just described.

---

*Note the profusion of names: Lord Edam, the Earl of Chetney, as well as Lord Arthur Chetney. There's something wrong with the names. If the father were a marquess and the title name is Edam, it would be proper to refer to him as "Lord Edam." We aren't told the family name, and Lord Edam's full name would be something like "William Smith, Marquess of Edam." Marquesses often had secondary titles. For example, William Smith might also be the Earl of Chetney. His eldest son—not yet the possessor of his father's hereditary title—would be properly titled something like "Henry Smith, Earl of Chetney" (without the "the") and familiarly referred to as Lord Chetney. The younger brother would not bear any title but would be given the honorific "Lord" or "the Honorable" before his family name, Arthur Smith, familiarly called "Lord Arthur" (never "Lord Chetney"), Davis, an American who presumably knew no better, improperly refers to the younger brother as "Lord Arthur Chetney." Note that the family lives in "Chetney House," suggesting that the earls of Chetney were a well-established lineage before Lord Edam was elevated to the rank of marquess.

"Apparently I had wandered very far in the fog, for up to noon to-day the house had not been found, nor had they been able to arrest Lord Arthur. He did not return to his father's house last night, and there is no trace of him; but from what the police knew of the past lives of the people I found in that lost house, they have evolved a theory, and their theory is that the murders were committed by Lord Arthur.

"The infatuation of his elder brother, Lord Chetney, for a Russian princess, so Inspector Lyle tells me, is well known to every one. About two years ago the Princess Zichy, as she calls herself, and he were constantly together, and Chetney informed his friends that they were about to be married. The woman was notorious in two continents, and when Lord Edam heard of his son's infatuation he appealed to the police for her record.

"It is through his having applied to them that they know so much concerning her and her relations with the Chetneys. From the police Lord Edam learned that Madame Zichy had once been a spy in the employ of the Russian Third Section,* but that lately she had been repudiated by her own government and was living by her wits, by blackmail, and by her beauty. Lord Edam laid this record before his son, but Chetney either knew it already or the woman persuaded him not to believe in it, and the father and son parted in great anger. Two days later the marquis altered his will, leaving all of his money to the younger brother, Arthur.

"The title and some of the landed property he could not keep from Chetney, but he swore if his son saw the woman again that the will should stand as it was, and he would be left without a penny.

"This was about eighteen months ago, when apparently Chetney tired of the Princess, and suddenly went off to shoot

---

*The intelligence and surveillance arm of the Imperial Chancellery of Russia—i.e., the czar's spy network.

and explore in Central Africa. No word came from him, except that twice he was reported as having died of fever in the jungle, and finally two traders reached the coast who said they had seen his body. This was accepted by all as conclusive, and young Arthur was recognized as the heir to the Edam millions. On the strength of this supposition he at once began to borrow enormous sums from the money lenders. This is of great importance, as the police believe it was these debts which drove him to the murder of his brother. Yesterday, as you know, Lord Chetney suddenly returned from the grave, and it was the fact that for two years he had been considered as dead which lent such importance to his return and which gave rise to those columns of detail concerning him which appeared in all the afternoon papers. But, obviously, during his absence he had not tired of the Princess Zichy, for we know that a few hours after he reached London he sought her out. His brother, who had also learned of his reappearance through the papers, probably suspected which would be the house he would first visit, and followed him there, arriving, so the Russian servant tells us, while the two were at coffee in the drawing-room. The Princess, then, we also learn from the servant, withdrew to the dining-room, leaving the brothers together. What happened one can only guess.

"Lord Arthur knew now that when it was discovered he was no longer the heir, the money lenders would come down upon him. The police believe that he at once sought out his brother to beg for money to cover the post-obits,[*] but that, considering the sum he needed was several hundreds of thousands of pounds,[†]

---

[*]A bond or promissory note payable on the death of a named person—here, upon the death of Lord Edam.

[†]One hundred thousand pounds in 1897 would be over 12 million pounds in 2023. Samuel H. Williamson, "Five Ways to Compute the Relative Value of a UK Pound Amount, 1270 to Present," Measuring Worth, 2023, https://www.measuringworth .com/calculators/ukcompare/relativevalue.php.

Chetney refused to give it him. No one knew that Arthur had gone to seek out his brother. They were alone. It is possible, then, that in a passion of disappointment, and crazed with the disgrace which he saw before him, young Arthur made himself the heir beyond further question. The death of his brother would have availed nothing if the woman remained alive. It is then possible that he crossed the hall, and with the same weapon which made him Lord Edam's heir destroyed the solitary witness to the murder. The only other person who could have seen it was sleeping in a drunken stupor, to which fact undoubtedly he owed his life. And yet," concluded the Naval Attaché, leaning forward and marking each word with his finger, "Lord Arthur blundered fatally. In his haste he left the door of the house open, so giving access to the first passer-by, and he forgot that when he entered it he had handed his card to the servant. That piece of paper may yet send him to the gallows. In the mean time he has disappeared completely, and somewhere, in one of the millions of streets of this great capital, in a locked and empty house, lies the body of his brother, and of the woman his brother loved, undiscovered, unburied, and with their murder unavenged."

In the discussion which followed the conclusion of the story of the Naval Attaché the gentleman with the pearl took no part. Instead, he arose, and, beckoning a servant to a far corner of the room, whispered earnestly to him until a sudden movement on the part of Sir Andrew caused him to return hurriedly to the table.

"There are several points in Mr. Sears's story I want explained," he cried. "Be seated, Sir Andrew," he begged. "Let us have the opinion of an expert. I do not care what the police think, I want to know what you think."

But Sir Henry* rose reluctantly from his chair.

---

*Evidently a typographical error—this is Sir Andrew speaking.

"I should like nothing better than to discuss this," he said. "But it is most important that I proceed to the House. I should have been there some time ago." He turned toward the servant and directed him to call a hansom.

The gentleman with the pearl stud looked appealingly at the Naval Attaché. "There are surely many details that you have not told us," he urged. "Some you have forgotten."

The Baronet interrupted quickly.

"I trust not," he said, "for I could not possibly stop to hear them."

"The story is finished," declared the Naval Attaché; "until Lord Arthur is arrested or the bodies are found there is nothing more to tell of either Chetney or the Princess Zichy."

"Of Lord Chetney perhaps not," interrupted the sporting-looking gentleman with the black tie, "but there'll always be something to tell of the Princess Zichy. I know enough stories about her to fill a book. She was a most remarkable woman." The speaker dropped the end of his cigar into his coffee cup and, taking his case from his pocket, selected a fresh one. As he did so he laughed and held up the case that the others might see it. It was an ordinary cigar-case of well-worn pigskin, with a silver clasp.

"The only time I ever met her," he said, "she tried to rob me of this."

The Baronet regarded him closely.

"She tried to rob you?" he repeated.

"Tried to rob me of this," continued the gentleman in the black tie, "and of the Czarina's diamonds." His tone was one of mingled admiration and injury.

"The Czarina's diamonds!" exclaimed the Baronet. He glanced quickly and suspiciously at the speaker, and then at the others about the table. But their faces gave evidence of no other emotion than that of ordinary interest.

"The Princess Zichy."

"Yes, the Czarina's diamonds," repeated the man with the black tie. "It was a necklace of diamonds. I was told to take them to the Russian Ambassador in Paris who was to deliver them at Moscow. I am a Queen's Messenger," he added.*

"Oh, I see," exclaimed Sir Andrew in a tone of relief. "And you say that this same Princess Zichy, one of the victims of this double murder, endeavored to rob you of—of—that cigar-case."

"And the Czarina's diamonds," answered the Queen's Messenger imperturbably. "It's not much of a story, but it gives you an idea of the woman's character. The robbery took place between Paris and Marseilles."

---

*A courier employed by the British Foreign Office to carry secret or important documents abroad, usually to embassies.

The Baronet interrupted him with an abrupt movement. "No, no," he cried, shaking his head in protest. "Do not tempt me. I really cannot listen. I must be at the House in ten minutes."

"I am sorry," said the Queen's Messenger. He turned to those seated about him. "I wonder if the other gentlemen—" he inquired tentatively. There was a chorus of polite murmurs, and the Queen's Messenger, bowing his head in acknowledgment, took a preparatory sip from his glass. At the same moment the servant to whom the man with the black pearl had spoken, slipped a piece of paper into his hand. He glanced at it, frowned, and threw it under the table.

The servant bowed to the Baronet.

"Your hansom is waiting, Sir Andrew," he said.

"The necklace was worth twenty thousand pounds," began the Queen's Messenger. "It was a present from the Queen of England to celebrate—" The Baronet gave an exclamation of angry annoyance.

"Upon my word, this is most provoking," he interrupted. "I really ought not to stay. But I certainly mean to hear this." He turned irritably to the servant. "Tell the hansom to wait," he commanded, and, with an air of a boy who is playing truant, slipped guiltily into his chair.

The gentleman with the black pearl smiled blandly, and rapped upon the table.

"Order, gentlemen," he said. "Order for the story of the Queen's Messenger and the Czarina's diamonds."

CHAPTER II

"The necklace was a present from the Queen of England to the Czarina of Russia," began the Queen's Messenger. "It was to celebrate the occasion of the Czar's coronation.* Our Foreign Office knew that the Russian Ambassador in Paris was to proceed to Moscow for that ceremony, and I was directed to go to Paris and turn over the necklace to him. But when I reached Paris I found he had not expected me for a week later and was taking a few days' vacation at Nice. His people asked me to leave the necklace with them at the embassy, but I had been charged to get a receipt for it from the Ambassador himself, so I started at once for Nice. The fact that Monte Carlo is not two thousand miles from Nice† may have had something to do with making me carry out my instructions so carefully.

"Now, how the Princess Zichy came to find out about the necklace I don't know, but I can guess. As you have just heard, she was at one time a spy in the service of the Russian government. And after they dismissed her she kept up her acquaintance

*The coronation took place on May 26, 1896.

†Moscow is about two thousand miles from Nice. Monte Carlo is about ten miles from Nice.

with many of the Russian agents in London. It is probable that through one of them she learned that the necklace was to be sent to Moscow, and which one of the Queen's Messengers had been detailed to take it there. Still, I doubt if even that knowledge would have helped her if she had not also known something which I supposed no one else in the world knew but myself and one other man. And, curiously enough, the other man was a Queen's Messenger too, and a friend of mine. You must know that up to the time of this robbery I had always concealed my despatches in a manner peculiarly my own. I got the idea from that play called 'A Scrap of Paper.'* In it a man wants to hide a certain compromising document. He knows that all his rooms will be secretly searched for it, so he puts it in a torn envelope and sticks it up where any one can see it on his mantel shelf. The result is that the woman who is ransacking the house to find it looks in all the unlikely places, but passes over the scrap of paper that is just under her nose. Sometimes the papers and packages they give us to carry about Europe are of very great value, and sometimes they are special makes of cigarettes, and orders to court dressmakers. Sometimes we know what we are carrying and sometimes we do not. If it is a large sum of money or a treaty, they generally tell us. But, as a rule, we have no knowledge of what the package contains; so, to be on the safe side, we naturally take just as great care of it as though we knew it held the terms of an ultimatum or the crown jewels. As a rule, my confrères carry the official packages in a despatch-box, which is just as obvious as a lady's jewel bag in the hands of her maid. Every one knows they are carrying something of value. They put a premium on dishonesty. Well, after I saw the 'Scrap

---

**Les Pattes de mouche* (*A Scrap of Paper*) by Victorien Sardou was a popular play first performed in 1860. Of course, the idea was used earlier by Edgar Allan Poe in "The Purloined Letter" (1844).

of Paper' play, I determined to put the government valuables in the most unlikely place that any one would look for them. So I used to hide the documents they gave me inside my riding-boots, and small articles, such as money or jewels, I carried in an old cigar-case. After I took to using my case for that purpose I bought a new one, exactly like it, for my cigars. But to avoid mistakes, I had my initials placed on both sides of the new one, and the moment I touched the case, even in the dark, I could tell which it was by the raised initials.

"No one knew of this except the Queen's Messenger of whom I spoke. We once left Paris together on the Orient Express. I was going to Constantinople and he was to stop off at Vienna. On the journey I told him of my peculiar way of hiding things and showed him my cigar-case. If I recollect rightly, on that trip it held the grand cross of St. Michael and St. George, which the Queen was sending to our Ambassador.* The Messenger was very much entertained at my scheme, and some months later when he met the Princess he told her about it as an amusing story. Of course, he had no idea she was a Russian spy. He didn't know anything at all about her, except that she was a very attractive woman. It was indiscreet, but he could not possibly have guessed that she could ever make any use of what he told her.

"Later, after the robbery, I remembered that I had informed this young chap of my secret hiding-place, and when I saw him again I questioned him about it. He was greatly distressed, and said he had never seen the importance of the secret. He remembered he had told several people of it, and among others the Princess Zichy. In that way I found out that it was she who had robbed me, and I know that from the moment I left London

---

*A collar of the Order of St. Michael and St. George with Grand Cross is a medal awarded to individuals who perform extraordinary services abroad on behalf of the United Kingdom—such as, apparently, the ambassador in Constantinople.

she was following me and that she knew then that the diamonds were concealed in my cigar-case.

"My train for Nice left Paris at ten in the morning. When I travel at night I generally tell the *chef de gare*[*] that I am a Queen's Messenger, and he gives me a compartment to myself, but in the daytime I take whatever offers. On this morning I had found an empty compartment, and I had tipped the guard to keep every one else out, not from any fear of losing the diamonds, but because I wanted to smoke. He had locked the door, and as the last bell had rung I supposed I was to travel alone, so I began to arrange my traps and make myself comfortable. The diamonds in the cigar-case were in the inside pocket of my waistcoat, and as they made a bulky package, I took them out, intending to put them in my hand bag. It is a small satchel like a bookmaker's, or those hand bags that couriers carry. I wear it slung from a strap across my shoulder, and, no matter whether I am sitting or walking, it never leaves me.

"I took the cigar-case which held the necklace from my inside pocket and the case which held the cigars out of the satchel, and while I was searching through it for a box of matches I laid the two cases beside me on the seat.

"At that moment the train started, but at the same instant there was a rattle at the lock of the compartment, and a couple of porters lifted and shoved a woman through the door, and hurled her rugs and umbrellas in after her.

"Instinctively I reached for the diamonds. I shoved them quickly into the satchel and, pushing them far down to the bottom of the bag, snapped the spring lock. Then I put the cigars in the pocket of my coat, but with the thought that now that I had a woman as a travelling companion I would probably not be allowed to enjoy them.

---

*The stationmaster.

"One of her pieces of luggage had fallen at my feet, and a roll of rugs had landed at my side. I thought if I hid the fact that the lady was not welcome, and at once endeavored to be civil, she might permit me to smoke. So I picked her hand bag off the floor and asked her where I might place it.

"As I spoke I looked at her for the first time, and saw that she was a most remarkably handsome woman.

"She smiled charmingly and begged me not to disturb myself. Then she arranged her own things about her, and, opening her dressing-bag, took out a gold cigarette-case.

"'Do you object to smoke?' she asked.

"I laughed and assured her I had been in great terror lest she might object to it herself.

"'If you like cigarettes,' she said, 'will you try some of these? They are rolled especially for my husband in Russia, and they are supposed to be very good.'

"I thanked her, and took one from her case, and I found it so much better than my own that I continued to smoke her cigarettes throughout the rest of the journey. I must say that we got on very well. I judged from the coronet on her cigarette-case, and from her manner, which was quite as well bred as that of any woman I ever met, that she was some one of importance, and though she seemed almost too good looking to be respectable, I determined that she was some *grande dame* who was so assured of her position that she could afford to be unconventional. At first she read her novel, and then she made some comment on the scenery, and finally we began to discuss the current politics of the Continent. She talked of all the cities in Europe, and seemed to know every one worth knowing. But she volunteered nothing about herself except that she frequently made use of the expression, 'When my husband was stationed at Vienna,' or 'When my husband was promoted to Rome.' Once she said to me, 'I have often seen you at Monte Carlo. I saw you when you won the pigeon championship.' I told her that I was not a pigeon shot, and she gave a little start of surprise. 'Oh, I beg your pardon,' she said; 'I thought you were Morton Hamilton, the English champion.' As a matter of fact, I do look like Hamilton, but I know now that her object was to make me think that she had no idea as to who I really was. She needn't have acted at all, for I certainly had no suspicions of her, and was only too pleased to have so charming a companion.

"The one thing that should have made me suspicious was the fact that at every station she made some trivial excuse to get me out of the compartment. She pretended that her maid was travelling back of us in one of the second-class carriages, and kept saying she could not imagine why the woman did not come to look after her, and if the maid did not turn up at the next stop, would I be so very kind as to get out and bring her whatever it was she pretended she wanted.

"I had taken my dressing-case from the rack to get out a novel, and had left it on the seat opposite to mine, and at the end of the compartment farthest from her. And once when I came back from buying her a cup of chocolate, or from some other fool errand, I found her standing at my end of the compartment with both hands on the dressing-bag. She looked at me without so much as winking an eye, and shoved the case carefully into a corner. 'Your bag slipped off on the floor,' she said. 'If you've got any bottles in it, you had better look and see that they're not broken.'

"And I give you my word, I was such an ass that I did open the case and looked all through it. She must have thought I *was* a Juggins.* I get hot all over whenever I remember it. But in spite of my dulness, and her cleverness, she couldn't gain anything by

---

*A simpleton or fool. According to the Oxford English Dictionary, the name refers to the character "Juggins" in Benjamin Disraeli's 1845 novel *Sybil, or The Two Nations*.

sending me away, because what she wanted was in the hand bag and every time she sent me away the hand bag went with me.

"After the incident of the dressing-case her manner changed. Either in my absence she had had time to look through it, or, when I was examining it for broken bottles, she had seen everything it held.

"From that moment she must have been certain that the cigar-case, in which she knew I carried the diamonds, was in the bag that was fastened to my body, and from that time on she probably was plotting how to get it from me.

"Her anxiety became most apparent. She dropped the great lady manner, and her charming condescension went with it. She ceased talking, and, when I spoke, answered me irritably, or at random. No doubt her mind was entirely occupied with her plan. The end of our journey was drawing rapidly nearer, and her time for action was being cut down with the speed of the express train. Even I, unsuspicious as I was, noticed that something was very wrong with her. I really believe that before we reached Marseilles if I had not, through my own stupidity, given her the chance she wanted, she might have stuck a knife in me and rolled me out on the rails. But as it was, I only thought that the long journey had tired her. I suggested that it was a very trying trip, and asked her if she would allow me to offer her some of my cognac.

"She thanked me and said, 'No,' and then suddenly her eyes lighted, and she exclaimed, 'Yes, thank you, if you will be so kind.'

"My flask was in the hand bag, and I placed it on my lap and with my thumb slipped back the catch. As I keep my tickets and railroad guide in the bag, I am so constantly opening it that I never bother to lock it, and the fact that it is strapped to me has always been sufficient protection. But I can appreciate now what a satisfaction, and what a torment too, it must have been to that woman when she saw that the bag opened without a key.

"While we were crossing the mountains I had felt rather chilly and had been wearing a light racing coat. But after the lamps were lighted the compartment became very hot and stuffy, and I found the coat uncomfortable. So I stood up, and, after first slipping the strap of the bag over my head, I placed the bag in the seat next to me and pulled off the racing coat. I don't blame myself for being careless; the bag was still within reach of my hand, and nothing would have happened if at that exact moment the train had not stopped at Arles. It was the combination of my removing the bag and our entering the station at the same instant which gave the Princess Zichy the chance she wanted to rob me.

"This gave the Princess Zichy the chance she wanted to rob me."

"I needn't say that she was clever enough to take it. The train ran into the station at full speed and came to a sudden stop. I had just thrown my coat into the rack, and had reached out my hand for the bag. In another instant I would have had the strap around my shoulder. But at that moment the Princess threw open the door of the compartment and beckoned wildly at the people on the platform. 'Natalie!' she called, 'Natalie! here I am. Come here! This way!' She turned upon me in the greatest excitement. 'My maid!' she cried. 'She is looking for me. She passed the window without seeing me. Go, please, and bring her back.' She continued pointing out of the door and beckoning me with her other hand. There certainly was something about that woman's tone which made one jump. When she was giving orders you had no chance to think of anything else. So I rushed out on my errand of mercy, and then rushed back again to ask what the maid looked like.

"In black,' she answered, rising and blocking the door of the compartment. 'All in black, with a bonnet!'

"The train waited three minutes at Arles, and in that time I suppose I must have rushed up to over twenty women and asked, 'Are you Natalie?' The only reason I wasn't punched with an umbrella or handed over to the police was that they probably thought I was crazy.

"When I jumped back into the compartment the Princess was seated where I had left her, but her eyes were burning with happiness. She placed her hand on my arm almost affection- ately, and said in a hysterical way, 'You are very kind to me. I am so sorry to have troubled you.'

"I protested that every woman on the platform was dressed in black.

"'Indeed I am so sorry,' she said, laughing; and she continued to laugh until she began to breathe so quickly that I thought she was going to faint.

"She knew she would be twenty thousand pounds richer."

"I can see now that the last part of that journey must have been a terrible half hour for her. She had the cigar-case safe enough, but she knew that she herself was not safe. She understood if I were to open my bag, even at the last minute, and miss the case, I would know positively that she had taken it. I had placed the diamonds in the bag at the very moment she entered the compartment, and no one but our two selves had occupied it since. She knew that when we reached Marseilles she would either be twenty thousand pounds richer than when she left Paris, or that she would go to jail. That was the situation as she must have read it, and I don't envy her her state of mind during that last half hour. It must have been hell.

"I saw that something was wrong, and in my innocence I even wondered if possibly my cognac had not been a little too

strong. For she suddenly developed into a most brilliant con-
versationalist, and applauded and laughed at everything I said,
and fired off questions at me like a machine gun, so that I had no
time to think of anything but of what she was saying. Whenever
I stirred she stopped her chattering and leaned toward me, and
watched me like a cat over a mouse-hole. I wondered how I
could have considered her an agreeable travelling companion.
I thought I would have preferred to be locked in with a lunatic.
I don't like to think how she would have acted if I had made a
move to examine the bag, but as I had it safely strapped around
me again, I did not open it, and I reached Marseilles alive. As we
drew into the station she shook hands with me and grinned at
me like a Cheshire cat.

"'I cannot tell you,' she said, 'how much I have to thank you
for.' What do you think of that for impudence?

"I offered to put her in a carriage, but she said she must find
Natalie, and that she hoped we would meet again at the hotel.
So I drove off by myself, wondering who she was, and whether
Natalie was not her keeper.

"I had to wait several hours for the train to Nice, and as I
wanted to stroll around the city I thought I had better put the
diamonds in the safe of the hotel. As soon as I reached my
room I locked the door, placed the hand bag on the table and
opened it. I felt among the things at the top of it, but failed to
touch the cigar-case. I shoved my hand in deeper, and stirred
the things about, but still I did not reach it. A cold wave swept
down my spine, and a sort of emptiness came to the pit of my
stomach. Then I turned red-hot, and the sweat sprung out
all over me. I wet my lips with my tongue, and said to myself,
'Don't be an ass. Pull yourself together, pull yourself together.
Take the things out, one at a time. It's there, of course it's there.
Don't be an ass.'

"I rushed across the room and threw out everything on the bed."

"So I put a brake on my nerves and began very carefully to pick out the things one by one, but after another second I could not stand it, and I rushed across the room and threw out everything on the bed. But the diamonds were not among them. I pulled the things about and tore them open and shuffled and rearranged and sorted them, but it was no use. The cigar-case was gone. I threw everything in the dressing-case out on the floor, although I knew it was useless to look for it there. I knew that I had put it in the bag. I sat down and tried to think. I remembered I had put it in the satchel at Paris just as that woman had entered the compartment, and I had been alone with her ever since, so it was she who had robbed me.

But how! It had never left my shoulder. And then I remembered that it had—that I had taken it off when I had changed my coat and for the few moments that I was searching for Natalie. I remembered that the woman had sent me on that goose chase, and that at every other station she had tried to get rid of me on some fool errand.

"I gave a roar like a mad bull, and I jumped down the stairs six steps at a time.

"I demanded at the office if a distinguished lady of title, possibly a Russian, had just entered the hotel.

"As I expected, she had not. I sprang into a cab and inquired at two other hotels, and then I saw the folly of trying to catch her without outside help, and I ordered the fellow to gallop to the office of the Chief of Police. I told my story, and the ass in charge asked me to calm myself, and wanted to take notes. I told him this was no time for taking notes, but for doing something. He got wrathy at that, and I demanded to be taken at once to his Chief. The Chief, he said, was very busy, and could not see me. So I showed him my silver greyhound.* In eleven years I had never used it but once before. I stated in pretty vigorous language that I was a Queen's Messenger, and that if the Chief of Police did not see me instantly he would lose his official head. At that the fellow jumped off his high horse and ran with me to his Chief,—a smart young chap, a colonel in the army, and a very intelligent man.

"I explained that I had been robbed in a French railway carriage of a diamond necklace belonging to the Queen of England, which her Majesty was sending as a present to the Czarina of Russia. I pointed out to him that if he succeeded

---

*The emblem of a badge worn by a messenger of the Foreign Office.

in capturing the thief he would be made for life, and would receive the gratitude of three great powers.

"He wasn't the sort that thinks second thoughts are best. He saw Russian and French decorations sprouting all over his chest, and he hit a bell, and pressed buttons, and yelled out orders like the captain of a penny steamer in a fog. He sent her description to all the city gates, and ordered all cabmen and railway porters to search all trains leaving Marseilles. He ordered all passengers on outgoing vessels to be examined, and telegraphed the proprietors of every hotel and pension to send him a complete list of their guests within the hour. While I was standing there he must have given at least a hundred orders, and sent out enough commissaires, sergeants de ville, gendarmes, bicycle police, and plain-clothes Johnnies to have captured the entire German army.* When they had gone he assured me that the woman was as good as arrested already. Indeed, officially, she was arrested; for she had no more chance of escape from Marseilles than from the Chateau D'If.†

"He told me to return to my hotel and possess my soul in peace. Within an hour he assured me he would acquaint me with her arrest.

"I thanked him, and complimented him on his energy, and left him. But I didn't share in his confidence. I felt that she was a very clever woman, and a match for any and all of us. It was all very well for him to be jubilant. He had not lost the diamonds, and had everything to gain if he found them; while I, even if he

---

*Commissaires are officers of the French National Police; sergeants de ville (the first uniformed police officers in the world, according to the French) are the equivalent of sergeants, supervising the gendarmes (the lowest-ranking police officials). The speaker here is simply rattling off titles, rather than being specific, suggesting that this was an "all hands on deck" matter for the police.

---

†A grim and foreboding island prison off the coast of Marseilles and, famously, the place of incarceration of Edmond Dantès, the Count of Monte Cristo, the hero of Alexandre Dumas's eponymous novel of 1844.

did recover the necklace, would only be where I was before I lost them, and if he did not recover it I was a ruined man. It was an awful facer for me. I had always prided myself on my record. In eleven years I had never mislaid an envelope, nor missed taking the first train. And now I had failed in the most important mission that had ever been intrusted to me. And it wasn't a thing that could be hushed up, either. It was too conspicuous, too spectacular. It was sure to invite the widest notoriety. I saw myself ridiculed all over the Continent, and perhaps dismissed, even suspected of having taken the thing myself.

"I threw everything in the dressing-case out on the floor."

"I was walking in front of a lighted café, and I felt so sick and miserable that I stopped for a pick-me-up. Then I considered that if I took one drink I would probably, in my present state of mind, not want to stop under twenty, and I decided I had better leave it alone. But my nerves were jumping like a frightened rabbit, and I felt I must have something to quiet them, or I would go crazy. I reached for my cigarette-case, but a cigarette seemed hardly adequate, so I put it back again and took out this cigar-case, in which I keep only the strongest and blackest cigars. I opened it and stuck in my fingers, but instead of a cigar they touched on a thin leather envelope. My heart stood perfectly still. I did not dare to look, but I dug my finger nails into the leather and I felt layers of thin paper, then a layer of cotton, and then they scratched on the facets of the Czarina's diamonds!

"I stumbled as though I had been hit in the face, and fell back into one of the chairs on the sidewalk. I tore off the wrappings and spread out the diamonds on the café table; I could not believe they were real. I twisted the necklace between my fingers and crushed it between my palms and tossed it up in the air. I believe I almost kissed it. The women in the café stood up on the chairs to see better, and laughed and screamed, and the people crowded so close around me that the waiters had to form a bodyguard. The proprietor thought there was a fight, and called for the police. I was so happy I didn't care. I laughed, too, and gave the proprietor a five-pound note, and told him to stand every one a drink. Then I tumbled into a fiacre* and galloped off to my friend the Chief of Police. I felt very sorry for him. He had been so happy at the chance I gave him, and he was sure to be disappointed when he learned I had sent him off on a false alarm.

---

*A small four-wheeled carriage, usually hired out to the public—i.e., the equivalent of a taxicab.

"But now that I had found the necklace, I did not want him to find the woman. Indeed, I was most anxious that she should get clear away, for if she were caught the truth would come out, and I was likely to get a sharp reprimand, and sure to be laughed at.

"I could see now how it had happened. In my haste to hide the diamonds when the woman was hustled into the carriage, I had shoved the cigars into the satchel, and the diamonds into the pocket of my coat. Now that I had the diamonds safe again, it seemed a very natural mistake. But I doubted if the Foreign Office would think so. I was afraid it might not appreciate the beautiful simplicity of my secret hiding-place. So, when I reached the police station, and found that the woman was still at large, I was more than relieved.

"As I expected, the Chief was extremely chagrined when he learned of my mistake, and that there was nothing for him to do. But I was feeling so happy myself that I hated to have any one else miserable, so I suggested that this attempt to steal the Czarina's necklace might be only the first of a series of such attempts by an unscrupulous gang, and that I might still be in danger.

"I winked at the Chief and the Chief smiled at me, and we went to Nice together in a saloon car with a guard of twelve carabineers and twelve plain-clothes men, and the Chief and I drank champagne all the way. We marched together up to the hotel where the Russian Ambassador was stopping, closely surrounded by our escort of carabineers, and delivered the necklace with the most profound ceremony. The old Ambassador was immensely impressed, and when we hinted that already I had been made the object of an attack by robbers, he assured us that his Imperial Majesty would not prove ungrateful.

"I wrote a swinging* personal letter about the invaluable services of the Chief to the French Minister of Foreign Affairs, and they gave him enough Russian and French medals to satisfy even a French soldier. So, though he never caught the woman, he received his just reward."

The Queen's Messenger paused and surveyed the faces of those about him in some embarrassment.

"But the worst of it is," he added, "that the story must have got about; for, while the Princess obtained nothing from me but a cigar-case and five excellent cigars, a few weeks after the coronation the Czar sent me a gold cigar-case with his monogram in diamonds. And I don't know yet whether that was a coincidence, or whether the Czar wanted me to know that he knew that I had been carrying the Czarina's diamonds in my pigskin cigar-case. What do you fellows think!"

---

*Slang meaning "of great size"—in this case, the Queen's Messenger speaks figuratively.

CHAPTER III

Sir Andrew rose with disapproval written in every lineament.

"I thought your story would bear upon the murder," he said. "Had I imagined it would have nothing whatsoever to do with it I would not have remained." He pushed back his chair and bowed stiffly. "I wish you good night," he said.

There was a chorus of remonstrance, and under cover of this and the Baronet's answering protests a servant for the second time slipped a piece of paper into the hand of the gentleman with the pearl stud. He read the lines written upon it and tore it into tiny fragments.

The youngest member, who had remained an interested but silent listener to the tale of the Queen's Messenger, raised his hand commandingly.

"Sir Andrew," he cried, "in justice to Lord Arthur Chetney I must ask you to be seated. He has been accused in our hearing of a most serious crime, and I insist that you remain until you have heard me clear his character."

"You!" cried the Baronet.

"Yes," answered the young man briskly. "I would have spoken sooner," he explained, "but that I thought this gentleman"—he inclined his head toward the Queen's Messenger—"was about to contribute some facts of which I was ignorant. He, however, has told us nothing, and so I will take up the tale at the point where Lieutenant Sears laid it down and give you those details of which Lieutenant Sears is ignorant. It seems strange to you that I should be able to add the sequel to this story. But the coincidence is easily explained. I am the junior member of the law firm of Chudleigh & Chudleigh. We have been solicitors for the Chetneys for the last two hundred years. Nothing, no matter how unimportant, which concerns Lord Edam and his two sons is unknown to us, and naturally we are acquainted with every detail of the terrible catastrophe of last night."

The Baronet, bewildered but eager, sank back into his chair.

"Will you be long, sir?" he demanded.

"I shall endeavor to be brief," said the young Solicitor; "and," he added, in a tone which gave his words almost the weight of a threat, "I promise to be interesting."

"There is no need to promise that," said Sir Andrew, "I find it much too interesting as it is." He glanced ruefully at the clock and turned his eyes quickly from it.

"Tell the driver of that hansom," he called to the servant, "that I take him by the hour."

"For the last three days," began young Mr. Chudleigh, "as you have probably read in the daily papers, the Marquis of Edam has been at the point of death, and his physicians have never left his house. Every hour he seemed to grow weaker; but although his bodily strength is apparently leaving him forever, his mind has remained clear and active. Late yesterday evening word was received at our office that he wished my father to come at once to Chetney House and to bring with him certain papers. What these papers were is not essential; I mention them only to explain how it was that last night I happened to be at Lord Edam's bedside. I accompanied my father to Chetney House, but at the time we reached there Lord Edam was sleeping, and his physicians refused to have him awakened. My father urged that he should be allowed to receive Lord Edam's instructions concerning the documents, but the physicians would not disturb him, and we all gathered in the library to wait until he should awake of his own accord. It was about one o'clock in the morning, while we were still there, that Inspector Lyle and the officers from Scotland Yard came to arrest Lord Arthur on the charge of murdering his brother. You can imagine our dismay and distress. Like every one else, I had learned from the afternoon papers that Lord Chetney was not dead, but that he had returned to England, and on arriving at Chetney House I had been told that Lord Arthur had gone to the Bath Hotel to look for his brother and to inform him that if he wished to see their father alive he must come to him at once. Although it was now past one o'clock, Arthur had not returned. None of us knew where Madame Zichy lived, so we could not go to recover Lord Chetney's body. We spent a most miserable night, hastening to the window whenever a cab came into the square, in the hope that it was Arthur returning, and endeavoring to explain away the facts that pointed to him as the murderer. I am a friend of Arthur's, I was with him at Harrow* and at Oxford, and I refused to believe for an instant that he was capable of such a crime; but as a lawyer I could not help but see that the circumstantial evidence was strongly against him.

"Toward early morning Lord Edam awoke, and in so much better a state of health that he refused to make the changes in

---

*Harrow is a "public school" (the equivalent of private school in America) of great antiquity and renown in London. The famous public school Eton claims priority, having been chartered by King Henry VI in 1440; it was not until 1572 that Harrow was chartered by Queen Elizabeth I. Until recently, most of the nation's prime ministers attended one or the other.

the papers which he had intended, declaring that he was no nearer death than ourselves. Under other circumstances, this happy change in him would have relieved us greatly, but none of us could think of anything save the death of his elder son and of the charge which hung over Arthur.

"As long as Inspector Lyle remained in the house my father decided that I, as one of the legal advisers of the family, should also remain there. But there was little for either of us to do. Arthur did not return, and nothing occurred until late this morning, when Lyle received word that the Russian servant had been arrested. He at once drove to Scotland Yard to question him. He came back to us in an hour, and informed me that the servant had refused to tell anything of what had happened the night before, or of himself, or of the Princess Zichy. He would not even give them the address of her house.

"'He is in abject terror,' Lyle said. 'I assured him that he was not suspected of the crime, but he would tell me nothing.'

"We found him propped up in bed with his head bound in a bandage."

"There were no other developments until two o'clock this afternoon, when word was brought to us that Arthur had been found, and that he was lying in the accident ward of St. George's Hospital.* Lyle and I drove there together, and found him propped up in bed with his head bound in a bandage. He had been brought to the hospital the night before by the driver of a hansom that had run over him in the fog. The cab-horse had kicked him on the head, and he had been carried in unconscious. There was nothing on him to tell who he was, and it was not until he came to his senses this afternoon that the hospital authorities had been able to send word to his people. Lyle at once informed him that he was under arrest, and with what he was charged, and though the inspector warned him to say nothing which might be used against him, I, as his solicitor, instructed him to speak freely and to tell us all he knew of the occurrences of last night. It was evident to any one that the fact of his brother's death was of much greater concern to him, than that he was accused of his murder.

"'That,' Arthur said contemptuously, 'that is damned nonsense. It is monstrous and cruel. We parted better friends than we have been in years. I will tell you all that happened—not to clear myself, but to help you to find out the truth.' His story is as follows: Yesterday afternoon, owing to his constant attendance on his father, he did not look at the evening papers, and it was not until after dinner, when the butler brought him one and told him of its contents, that he learned that his brother was alive and at the Bath Hotel. He drove there at once, but was told that about eight o'clock his brother had gone out, but without giving any clew to his destination. As Chetney had not at once come to see his father, Arthur decided that he was still angry

---

*The hospital, now in Tooting, was originally in Lanesborough House, at Hyde Park Corner, a very short walk from Knightsbridge.

with him, and his mind, turning naturally to the cause of their quarrel, determined him to look for Chetney at the home of the Princess Zichy.

"Her house had been pointed out to him, and though he had never visited it, he had passed it many times and knew its exact location. He accordingly drove in that direction, as far as the fog would permit the hansom to go, and walked the rest of the way, reaching the house about nine o'clock. He rang, and was admitted by the Russian servant. The man took his card into the drawing-room, and at once his brother ran out and welcomed him. He was followed by the Princess Zichy, who also received Arthur most cordially.

"'You brothers will have much to talk about,' she said. 'I am going to the dining-room. When you have finished, let me know.'

"As soon as she had left them, Arthur told his brother that their father was not expected to outlive the night, and that he must come to him at once.

"'This is not the moment to remember your quarrel,' Arthur said to him; 'you have come back from the dead only in time to make your peace with him before he dies.'

"Arthur says that at this Chetney was greatly moved.

"'You entirely misunderstand me, Arthur,' he returned. 'I did not know the governor was ill, or I would have gone to him the instant I arrived. My only reason for not doing so was because I thought he was still angry with me. I shall return with you immediately, as soon as I have said good-by to the Princess. It is a final good-by. After to-night, I shall never see her again.'

"'Do you mean that?' Arthur cried.

"'Yes,' Chetney answered. 'When I returned to London I had no intention of seeking her again, and I am here only through a mistake.' He then told Arthur that he had separated from the

Princess even before he went to Central Africa, and that, more-over, while at Cairo on his way south, he had learned certain facts concerning her life there during the previous season, which made it impossible for him to ever wish to see her again. Their separation was final and complete.

"'She deceived me cruelly,' he said; 'I cannot tell you how cruelly. During the two years when I was trying to obtain my father's consent to our marriage she was in love with a Russian diplomat. During all that time he was secretly visiting her here in London, and her trip to Cairo was only an excuse to meet him there.'

"'Yet you are here with her to-night,' Arthur protested, 'only a few hours after your return.'

"'That is easily explained,' Chetney answered. 'As I finished dinner to-night at the hotel, I received a note from her from this address. In it she said she had but just learned of my arrival, and begged me to come to her at once. She wrote that she was in great and present trouble, dying of an incurable illness, and without friends or money. She begged me, for the sake of old times, to come to her assistance. During the last two years in the jungle all my former feeling for Zichy has utterly passed away, but no one could have dismissed the appeal she made in that letter. So I came here, and found her, as you have seen her, quite as beautiful as she ever was, in very good health, and, from the look of the house, in no need of money.

"'I asked her what she meant by writing me that she was dying in a garret, and she laughed, and said she had done so because she was afraid, unless I thought she needed help, I would not try to see her. That was where we were when you arrived. And now,' Chetney added, 'I will say good-by to her, and you had better return home. No, you can trust me, I shall follow you at once. She has no influence over me now, but I believe, in spite of the way she has used me, that she is, after her queer fashion, still fond of me, and when she learns that this good-by is final there may be a scene, and it is not fair to her that you should be here. So, go home at once, and tell the governor that I am following you in ten minutes.'

"'That,' said Arthur, 'is the way we parted. I never left him on more friendly terms. I was happy to see him alive again, I was happy to think he had returned in time to make up his quarrel with my father, and I was happy that at last he was shut of that woman. I was never better pleased with him in my life.' He turned to Inspector Lyle, who was sitting at the foot of the bed taking notes of all he told us.

"'Why in the name of common sense,' he cried, 'should I have chosen that moment of all others to send my brother back to the grave?' For a moment the Inspector did not answer him. I do not know if any of you gentlemen are acquainted with Inspector Lyle, but if you are not, I can assure you that he is a very remarkable man. Our firm often applies to him for aid, and he has never failed us; my father has the greatest possible respect for him. Where he has the advantage over the ordinary police official is in the fact that he possesses imagination. He imagines himself to be the criminal, imagines how he would act under the same circumstances, and he imagines to such purpose that he generally finds the man he wants. I have often told Lyle that if he had not been a detective he would have made a great success as a poet, or a playwright.*

---

*Sherlock Holmes explains, "You'll get results, Inspector, by always putting yourself in the other fellow's place, and thinking what you would do yourself. It takes some imagination, but it pays." Arthur Conan Doyle, "The Retired Colourman," *The Complete Sherlock Holmes Short Stories* (London: John Murray, 1927), 1334. As Holmes puts it in *The Valley of Fear*, "And yet there should be no combination of events for which the wit of man cannot conceive an explanation. Simply as a mental exercise, without any assertion that it is true, let me indicate a possible line of thought. It is, I admit, mere imagination; but how often is imagination the mother of truth?" Arthur Conan Doyle,

"When Arthur turned on him Lyle hesitated for a moment, and then told him exactly what was the case against him.

"'Ever since your brother was reported as having died in Africa,' he said, 'your Lordship has been collecting money on post-obits. Lord Chetney's arrival last night turned them into waste paper. You were suddenly in debt for thousands of pounds—for much more than you could ever possibly pay. No one knew that you and your brother had met at Madame Zichy's. But you knew that your father was not expected to out-live the night, and that if your brother were dead also, you would be saved from complete ruin, and that you would become the Marquis of Edam.'

"'Oh, that is how you have worked it out, is it?' Arthur cried. 'And for me to become Lord Edam was it necessary that the woman should die, too?'

"'They will say,' Lyle answered, 'that she was a witness to the murder—that she would have told.'

"'Then why did I not kill the servant as well?' Arthur said.

"'He was asleep, and saw nothing.'

"'And you believe *that?*' Arthur demanded.

"'It is not a question of what I believe,' Lyle said gravely. 'It is a question for your peers.'

"'The man is insolent!' Arthur cried. 'The thing is monstrous! Horrible!'

"Before we could stop him he sprang out of his cot and began pulling on his clothes. When the nurses tried to hold him down, he fought with them.

"'Do you think you can keep me here,' he shouted, 'when they are plotting to hang me! I am going with you to that house!' he cried at Lyle. 'When you find those bodies I shall be beside you. It is my right. He is my brother. He has been murdered, and I can tell you who murdered him. That woman murdered him. She first ruined his life, and now she has killed him. For the last five years she has been plotting to make herself his wife, and last night, when he told her he had discovered the truth about the Russian, and that she would never see him again, she flew into a passion and stabbed him, and then, in terror of the gallows, killed herself. She murdered him, I tell you, and I promise you that we will find the knife she used near her—perhaps still in her hand. What will you say to that?'

"Lyle turned his head away and stared down at the floor. 'I might say,' he answered, 'that you placed it there.'

"Arthur gave a cry of anger and sprang at him, and then pitched forward into his arms. The blood was running from the cut under the bandage, and he had fainted. Lyle carried him back to the bed again, and we left him with the police and the doctors, and drove at once to the address he had given us. We found the house not three minutes' walk from St. George's Hospital. It stands in Trevor Terrace, that little row of houses set back from Knightsbridge, with one end in Hill Street.*

"As we left the hospital Lyle had said to me, 'You must not blame me for treating him as I did. All is fair in this work, and if by angering that boy I could have made him commit himself I was right in trying to do so; though, I assure you, no one would be better pleased than myself if I could prove his theory to be correct. But we cannot tell. Everything depends upon what we see for ourselves within the next few minutes.'

---

*In 1897, Trevor Terrace, a real street in Knightsbridge, had a music hall and a few shops on the eastern end, but on the western end, there were tall and substantial houses with front gardens of appreciable depth such as has been described. See *Survey of London: Volume 45, Knightsbridge* (London: London County Council, 2000).

"In the drawing-room, we found the body of the Princess Zichy."

"When we reached the house, Lyle broke open the fasten-ings of one of the windows on the ground floor, and, hidden by the trees in the garden, we scrambled in. We found ourselves in the reception-room, which was the first room on the right of the hall. The gas was still burning behind the colored glass and red silk shades, and when the daylight streamed in after us it gave the hall a hideously dissipated look, like the foyer of a theatre at a matinee, or the entrance to an all-day gambling hell. The house was oppressively silent, and because we knew why it was so silent we spoke in whispers. When Lyle turned the handle of the drawing-room door, I felt as though some one had put his hand upon my throat. But I followed close at his shoulder, and saw, in the subdued light of many-tinted lamps, the body of Chetney at the foot of the divan, just as Lieutenant Sears had described it. In the drawing-room we found the body of the Princess Zichy, her arms thrown out, and the blood from her heart frozen in a tiny line across her bare shoulder. But neither of us, although we searched the floor on our hands and knees, could find the weapon which had killed her.

"'For Arthur's sake,' I said, 'I would have given a thousand pounds if we had found the knife in her hand, as he said we would.'

"'That we have not found it there,' Lyle answered, 'is to my mind the strongest proof that he is telling the truth, that he left the house before the murder took place. He is not a fool, and had he stabbed his brother and this woman, he would have seen that by placing the knife near her he could help to make it appear as if she had killed Chetney and then committed suicide. Besides, Lord Arthur insisted that the evidence in his behalf would be our finding the knife here. He would not have urged that if he knew we would *not* find it, if he knew he himself had carried it away. This is no suicide. A suicide does not rise and hide the weapon with which he kills himself, and then lie down again. No, this has been a double murder, and we must look outside of the house for the murderer.'

"While he was speaking Lyle and I had been searching every corner, studying the details of each room. I was so afraid that, without telling me, he would make some deductions prejudicial to Arthur, that I never left his side. I was determined to see everything that he saw, and, if possible, to prevent his interpreting it in the wrong way. He finally finished his examination, and we sat down together in the drawing-room, and he took out his notebook and read aloud all that Mr. Sears had told him of the murder and what we had just learned from Arthur. We compared the two accounts word for word, and weighed statement with statement, but I could not determine from anything Lyle said which of the two versions he had decided to believe.

"'We are trying to build a house of blocks,' he exclaimed,

'with half of the blocks missing. We have been considering two theories,' he went on: 'one that Lord Arthur is responsible for both murders, and the other that the dead woman in there is responsible for one of them, and has committed suicide; but, until the Russian servant is ready to talk, I shall refuse to believe in the guilt of either.'

"'What can you prove by him?' I asked. 'He was drunk and asleep. He saw nothing.'

"Lyle hesitated, and then, as though he had made up his mind to be quite frank with me, spoke freely.

"'I do not know that he was either drunk or asleep,' he answered. 'Lieutenant Sears describes him as a stupid boor. I am not satisfied that he is not a clever actor. What was his position in this house? What was his real duty here? Suppose it was not to guard this woman, but to watch her. Let us imagine that it was not the woman he served, but a master, and see where that leads us. For this house has a master, a mysterious, absentee landlord, who lives in St. Petersburg, the unknown Russian who came between Chetney and Zichy, and because of whom Chetney left her. He is the man who bought this house for Madame Zichy, who sent these rugs and curtains from St. Petersburg to furnish it for her after his own tastes, and, I believe, it was he also who placed the Russian servant here, ostensibly to serve the Princess, but in reality to spy upon her. At Scotland Yard we do not know who this gentleman is; the Russian police confess to equal ignorance concerning him. When Lord Chetney went to Africa, Madame Zichy lived in St. Petersburg; but there her receptions and dinners were so crowded with members of the nobility and of the army and diplomats, that among so many visitors the police could not learn which was the one for whom she most greatly cared.'

"Lyle pointed at the modern French paintings and the heavy silk rugs which hung upon the walls.

"Entreating Chetney not to leave her."

"'The unknown is a man of taste and of some fortune,' he said, 'not the sort of man to send a stupid peasant to guard the woman he loves. So I am not content to believe, with Mr. Sears, that the servant is a boor. I believe him instead to be a very clever ruffian. I believe him to be the protector of his master's honor, or, let us say, of his master's property, whether that property be silver plate or the woman his master loves. Last night, after Lord

Arthur had gone away, the servant was left alone in this house with Lord Chetney and Madame Zichy. From where he sat in the hall he could hear Lord Chetney bidding her farewell; for, if my idea of him is correct, he understands English quite as well as you or I. Let us imagine that he heard her entreating Chetney not to leave her, reminding him of his former wish to marry her, and let us suppose that he hears Chetney denounce her, and tell her that at Cairo he has learned of this Russian admirer—the servant's master. He hears the woman declare that she has had no admirer but himself, that this unknown Russian was, and is, nothing to her, that there is no man she loves but him, and that she cannot live, knowing that he is alive, without his love. Suppose Chetney believed her, suppose his former infatuation for her returned, and that in a moment of weakness he forgave her and took her in his arms. That is the moment the Russian master has feared. It is to guard against it that he has placed his watchdog over the Princess, and how do we know but that, when the moment came, the watchdog served his master, as he saw his duty, and killed them both? What do you think?' Lyle demanded. 'Would not that explain both murders?'

"I was only too willing to hear any theory which pointed to any one else as the criminal than Arthur, but Lyle's explanation was too utterly fantastic. I told him that he certainly showed imagination, but that he could not hang a man for what he imagined he had done.

"'No,' Lyle answered, 'but I can frighten him by telling him what I think he has done, and now when I again question the Russian servant I will make it quite clear to him that I believe he is the murderer. I think that will open his mouth. A man will at least talk to defend himself. Come,' he said, 'we must return at once to Scotland Yard and see him. There is nothing more to do here.'

"He arose, and I followed him into the hall, and in another minute we would have been on our way to Scotland Yard. But just as he opened the street door a postman halted at the gate of the garden, and began fumbling with the latch.

"Lyle stopped, with an exclamation of chagrin.

"'How stupid of me!' he exclaimed. He turned quickly and pointed to a narrow slit cut in the brass plate of the front door. 'The house has a private letter-box,' he said, 'and I had not thought to look in it! If we had gone out as we came in, by the window, I would never have seen it. The moment I entered the house I should have thought of securing the letters which came this morning. I have been grossly careless.' He stepped back into the hall and pulled at the lid of the letter-box, which hung on the inside of the door, but it was tightly locked. At the same moment the postman came up the steps holding a letter. Without a word Lyle took it from his hand and began to exam ine it. It was addressed to the Princess Zichy, and on the back of the envelope was the name of a West End dressmaker.

"'That is of no use to me,' Lyle said. He took out his card and showed it to the postman. 'I am Inspector Lyle from Scotland Yard,' he said. 'The people in this house are under arrest. Everything it contains is now in my keeping. Did you deliver any other letters here this morning?'

"The man looked frightened, but answered promptly that he was now upon his third round. He had made one postal delivery at seven that morning and another at eleven.*

"'How many letters did you leave here?' Lyle asked.

"'About six altogether,' the man answered.

"'Did you put them through the door into the letter-box?'

"The postman said, 'Yes, I always slip them into the box, and ring and go away. The servants collect them from the inside.'

*Mail deliveries occurred as frequently as six times a day in London.

"'Have you noticed if any of the letters you leave here bear a Russian postage stamp?' Lyle asked.

"The man answered, 'Oh, yes, sir, a great many.'

"'From the same person, would you say?'

"'The writing seems to be the same,' the man answered. 'They come regularly about once a week—one of those I delivered this morning had a Russian postmark.'

"'That will do,' said Lyle eagerly. 'Thank you, thank you very much.'

"He ran back into the hall, and, pulling out his penknife, began to pick at the lock of the letter-box.

"'I have been supremely careless,' he said in great excitement. 'Twice before when people I wanted had flown from a house I have been able to follow them by putting a guard over their mail-box. These letters, which arrive regularly every week from Russia in the same handwriting, they can come but from one person. At least, we shall now know the name of the master of this house. Undoubtedly it is one of his letters that the man placed here this morning. We may make a most important discovery.'

"As he was talking he was picking at the lock with his knife, but he was so impatient to reach the letters that he pressed too heavily on the blade and it broke in his hand. I took a step backward and drove my heel into the lock, and burst it open. The lid flew back, and we pressed forward, and each ran his hand down into the letter-box. For a moment we were both too startled to move. The box was empty.

"I do not know how long we stood staring stupidly at each other, but it was Lyle who was the first to recover. He seized me by the arm and pointed excitedly into the empty box.

"'Do you appreciate what that means!' he cried. 'It means that some one has been here ahead of us. Some one has entered this house not three hours before we came, since eleven o'clock this morning.'

"'It was the Russian servant!' I exclaimed.

"'The Russian servant has been under arrest at Scotland Yard,' Lyle cried. 'He could not have taken the letters. Lord Arthur has been in his cot at the hospital. That is his alibi. There is some one else, some one we do not suspect, and that some one is the murderer. He came back here either to obtain those letters because he knew they would convict him, or to remove something he had left here at the time of the murder, something incriminating,—the weapon, perhaps, or some personal article; a cigarette-case, a handkerchief with his name upon it, or a pair of gloves. Whatever it was it must have been damning evidence against him to have made him take so desperate a chance.'

"'How do we know,' I whispered, 'that he is not hidden here now?'

"'No, I'll swear he is not,' Lyle answered. 'I may have bungled in some things, but I have searched this house thoroughly. Nevertheless,' he added, 'we must go over it again, from the cellar to the roof. We have the real clew now, and we must forget the others and work only it.' As he spoke he began again to search the drawing-room, turning over even the books on the tables and the music on the piano.

"'Whoever the man is,' he said over his shoulder, 'we know that he has a key to the front door and a key to the letter-box. That shows us he is either an inmate of the house or that he comes here when he wishes. The Russian says that he was the only servant in the house. Certainly we have found no evidence to show that any other servant slept here. There could be but one other person who would possess a key to the house and the letter-box—and he lives in St. Petersburg. At the time of the murder he was two thousand miles away.' Lyle interrupted himself suddenly with a sharp cry and turned upon me with his eyes flashing. 'But was he?' he cried. 'Was he? How do we know that last night he was not in London, in this very house when Zichy and Chetney met?'

"He stood staring at me without seeing me, muttering, and arguing with himself.

"'Don't speak to me,' he cried, as I ventured to interrupt him. 'I can see it now. It is all plain. It was not the servant, but his master, the Russian himself, and it was he who came back for the letters! He came back for them because he knew they would convict him. We must find them. We must have those letters. If we find the one with the Russian postmark, we shall have found the murderer.' He spoke like a madman, and as he spoke he ran around the room with one hand held out in front of him as you have seen a mind-reader at a theatre seeking for something hidden in the stalls. He pulled the old letters from the writing-desk, and ran them over as swiftly as a gambler deals out cards; he dropped on his knees before the fireplace and dragged out the dead coals with his bare fingers, and then with a low, worried cry, like a hound on a scent, he ran back to the waste-paper basket and, lifting the papers from it, shook them out upon the floor. Instantly he gave a shout of triumph, and, separating a number of torn pieces from the others, held them up before me.

"'Look!' he cried. 'Do you see! Here are five letters, torn across in two places. The Russian did not stop to read them, for, as you see, he has left them still sealed. I have been wrong. He did not return for the letters. He could not have known their value. He must have returned for some other reason, and, as he was leaving, saw the letter-box, and taking out the letters, held them together—so—and tore them twice across, and then, as the fire had gone out, tossed them into this basket. Look!' he cried, 'here in the upper corner of this piece is a Russian stamp. This is his own letter—unopened!'

"We examined the Russian stamp and found it had been cancelled in St. Petersburg four days ago. The back of the envelope bore the postmark of the branch station in upper Sloane Street, and was dated this morning. The envelope was of official blue paper and we had no difficulty in finding the two other parts of it. We drew the torn pieces of the letter from them and joined them together side by side. There were but two lines of writing, and this was the message: 'I leave Petersburg on the night train, and I shall see you at Trevor Terrace after dinner Monday evening.'

"'That was last night!' Lyle cried. 'He arrived twelve hours ahead of his letter—but it came in time—it came in time to hang him!'"

The Baronet struck the table with his hand.

"The name!" he demanded. "How was it signed! What was the man's name?"

The young Solicitor rose to his feet and, leaning forward, stretched out his arm. "There was no name," he cried. "The letter was signed with only two initials. But engraved at the top of the sheet was the man's address. That address was 'THE AMERICAN EMBASSY, ST. PETERSBURG, BUREAU OF THE NAVAL ATTACHÉ,' and the initials," he shouted, his voice rising into an exultant and bitter cry, "were those of the gentleman who sits opposite who told us that he was the first to find the murdered bodies, the Naval Attaché to Russia, Lieutenant Sears!"

A strained and awful hush followed the Solicitor's words, which seemed to vibrate like a twanging bowstring that had just hurled its bolt. Sir Andrew, pale and staring, drew away with an exclamation of repulsion. His eyes were fastened upon the Naval Attaché with fascinated horror. But the American emitted a sigh of great content, and sank comfortably into the arms of his chair. He clapped his hands softly together.

"Capital!" he murmured. "I give you my word I never guessed what you were driving at. You fooled *me*, I'll be hanged if you didn't—you certainly fooled me."

The man with the pearl stud leaned forward with a nervous gesture. "Hush! be careful!" he whispered. But at that instant, for the third time, a servant, hastening through the room, handed him a piece of paper which he scanned eagerly. The message on the paper read, "The light over the Commons is out. The House has risen."

The man with the black pearl gave a mighty shout, and tossed the paper from him upon the table.

"Hurrah!" he cried. "The House is up! We've won!" He caught up his glass, and slapped the Naval Attaché violently upon the shoulder. He nodded joyously at him, at the Solicitor, and at the Queen's Messenger. "Gentlemen, to you!" he cried; "my thanks and my congratulations!" He drank deep from the glass, and breathed forth a long sigh of satisfaction and relief.

"But I say," protested the Queen's Messenger, shaking his finger violently at the Solicitor, "that story won't do. You didn't play fair—and—and you talked so fast I couldn't make out what it was all about. I'll bet you that evidence wouldn't hold in a court of law—you couldn't hang a cat on such evidence. Your story is condemned tommy-rot. Now my story might have happened, my story bore the mark—"

In the joy of creation the story-tellers had forgotten their audience, until a sudden exclamation from Sir Andrew caused them to turn guiltily toward him. His face was knit with lines of anger, doubt, and amazement.

"What does this mean?" he cried. "Is this a jest, or are you mad? If you know this man is a murderer, why is he at large! Is this a game you have been playing? Explain yourselves at once. What does it mean?"

The American, with first a glance at the others, rose and bowed courteously.

"I am not a murderer, Sir Andrew, believe me," he said; "you need not be alarmed. As a matter of fact, at this moment I am much more afraid of you than you could possibly be of me. I beg you please to be indulgent. I assure you, we meant no disrespect. We have been matching stories, that is all, pretending that we are people we are not, endeavoring to entertain you with better detective tales than, for instance, the last one you read, 'The Great Rand Robbery.'"

The Baronet brushed his hand nervously across his forehead.

"Do you mean to tell me," he exclaimed, "that none of this has happened? That Lord Chetney is not dead, that his Solicitor did not find a letter of yours written from your post in Petersburg, and that just now, when he charged you with murder, he was in jest?"

"I am really very sorry," said the American, "but you see, sir, he could not have found a letter written by me in St. Petersburg because I have never been in Petersburg. Until this week, I have never been outside of my own country. I am not a naval officer. I am a writer of short stories.* And to-night, when this gentleman told me that you were fond of detective stories, I thought it would be amusing to tell you one of my own—one I had just mapped out this afternoon."

"But Lord Chetney *is* a real person," interrupted the Baronet, "and he did go to Africa two years ago, and he was supposed to have died there, and his brother, Lord Arthur, has been the heir. And yesterday Chetney did return. I read it in the papers."

---

*Richard Harding Davis was himself an American writer of short stories. Though he went on to spend a good deal of time as a war correspondent during the Second Boer War (in South Africa) and the Spanish-American War (in Puerto Rico and Cuba), those adventures were after 1897.

"So did I," assented the American soothingly; "and it struck me as being a very good plot for a story. I mean his unexpected return from the dead, and the probable disappointment of the younger brother. So I decided that the younger brother had better murder the older one. The Princess Zichy I invented out of a clear sky. The fog I did not have to invent. Since last night I know all that there is to know about a London fog. I was lost in one for three hours."

The Baronet turned grimly upon the Queen's Messenger.

"But this gentleman," he protested, "he is not a writer of short stories; he is a member of the Foreign Office. I have often seen him in Whitehall, and, according to him, the Princess Zichy is not an invention. He says she is very well known, that she tried to rob him."

The servant of the Foreign Office looked unhappily at the Cabinet Minister, and puffed nervously on his cigar.

"It's true, Sir Andrew, that I am a Queen's Messenger," he said appealingly, "and a Russian woman once did try to rob a Queen's Messenger in a railway carriage—only it did not happen to me, but to a pal of mine. The only Russian princess I ever knew called herself Zabrisky. You may have seen her. She used to do a dive from the roof of the Aquarium."*

Sir Andrew, with a snort of indignation, fronted the young Solicitor.

"And I suppose yours was a cock-and-bull story, too," he said. "Of course, it must have been, since Lord Chetney is not dead. But don't tell me," he protested, "that you are not Chudleigh's son either."

"I'm sorry," said the youngest member, smiling in some

---

*More properly, the Royal Aquarium and Winter Garden, the "Aq," as it was popularly known, was a place of varied entertainments, including such spectacular and dangerous circus acts as the young female human cannonball, Zazel. There is no extant record of "Princess" Zabrisky performing there.

embarrassment, "but my name is not Chudleigh. I assure you, though, that I know the family very well, and that I am on very good terms with them."

"You should be!" exclaimed the Baronet; "and, judging from the liberties you take with the Chetneys, you had better be on very good terms with them, too."

The young man leaned back and glanced toward the servants at the far end of the room.

"It has been so long since I have been in the Club," he said, "that I doubt if even the waiters remember me. Perhaps Joseph may," he added. "Joseph!" he called, and at the word a servant stepped briskly forward.

The young man pointed to the stuffed head of a great lion which was suspended above the fireplace.

"Joseph," he said, "I want you to tell these gentlemen who shot that lion. Who presented it to the Grill?"

Joseph, unused to acting as master of ceremonies to members of the Club, shifted nervously from one foot to the other.

"Why, you—you did," he stammered.

"Of course I did!" exclaimed the young man. "I mean, what is the name of the man who shot it? Tell the gentlemen who I am. They wouldn't believe me."

"Who you are, my lord?" said Joseph. "You are Lord Edam's son, the Earl of Chetney."*

"You must admit," said Lord Chetney, when the noise had died away, "that I couldn't remain dead while my little brother was accused of murder. I had to do something. Family pride demanded it. Now, Arthur, as the younger brother, can't afford to be squeamish, but personally I should hate to have a brother of mine hanged for murder."

---

*The "the" is incorrect—see note on page 31, above. He would be, e.g., William Smith, Earl of Chetney or "Lord Chetney."

"You certainly showed no scruples against hanging me," said the American, "but in the face of your evidence I admit my guilt, and I sentence myself to pay the full penalty of the law as we are made to pay it in my own country. The order of this court is," he announced, "that Joseph shall bring me a wine-card, and that I sign it for five bottles of the Club's best champagne."

"Oh, no!" protested the man with the pearl stud, "it is not for *you* to sign it. In my opinion it is Sir Andrew who should pay the costs. It is time you knew," he said, turning to that gentleman, "that unconsciously you have been the victim of what I may call a patriotic conspiracy. These stories have had a more serious purpose than merely to amuse. They have been told with the worthy object of detaining you from the House of Commons. I must explain to you, that all through this evening I have had a servant waiting in Trafalgar Square with instructions to bring me word as soon as the light over the House of Commons had ceased to burn. The light is now out, and the object for which we plotted is attained."

The Baronet glanced keenly at the man with the black pearl, and then quickly at his watch. The smile disappeared from his lips, and his face was set in stern and forbidding lines.

"And may I know," he asked icily, "what was the object of your plot?"

"A most worthy one," the other retorted. "Our object was to keep you from advocating the expenditure of many millions of the people's money upon more battleships. In a word, we have been working together to prevent you from passing the Navy Increase Bill."

Sir Andrew's face bloomed with brilliant color. His body shook with suppressed emotion.

"What was the object of your plot?"

"My dear sir!" he cried, "you should spend more time at the House and less at your Club. The Navy Bill was brought up on its third reading at eight o'clock this evening. I spoke for three hours in its favor. My only reason for wishing to return again to the House to-night was to sup on the terrace with my old friend, Admiral Simons; for my work at the House was completed five hours ago, when the Navy Increase Bill was passed by an over-whelming majority."

The Baronet rose and bowed. "I have to thank you, sir," he said, "for a most interesting evening."

The American shoved the wine-card which Joseph had given him toward the gentleman with the black pearl.

"You sign it," he said.

THE END.

GALLEGHER: A NEWSPAPER STORY*

"Why, it's Gallegher!" said the night editor.

*Rejected by *The Century* (and according to some, a number of other lesser magazines), Davis sold this story to *Scribner's Magazine* in March 1890 for the lofty sum of $175, and it appeared in the August 1890 issue. However, it is likely that Davis started the story long before; in the summer of 1888, Davis's mother asked him how the work was coming (Davis, ed., *Adventures and Letters of Richard Harding Davis*, 40).

We had had so many office-boys before Gallegher came among us that they had begun to lose the characteristics of individuals, and became merged in a composite photograph of small boys, to whom we applied the generic title of "Here, you"; or "You, boy."

We had had sleepy boys, and lazy boys, and bright, "smart" boys, who became so familiar on so short an acquaintance that we were forced to part with them to save our own self-respect.

They generally graduated into district-messenger boys,* and occasionally returned to us in blue coats with nickel-plated buttons, and patronized us.

But Gallegher was something different from anything we had experienced before. Gallegher was short and broad in build, with a solid, muscular broadness, and not a fat and dumpy shortness. He wore perpetually on his face a happy and knowing smile, as if you and the world in general were not impressing him as seriously as you thought you were, and his eyes, which were very black and very bright, snapped intelligently at you like those of a little black-and-tan terrier.

All Gallegher knew had been learnt on the streets; not a very good school in itself, but one that turns out very knowing scholars. And Gallegher had attended both morning and evening sessions. He could not tell you who the Pilgrim Fathers were, nor could he name the thirteen original States, but he knew all the officers of the twenty-second police district by name, and he could distinguish the clang of a fire-engine's gong from that of a patrol-wagon or an ambulance fully two blocks distant. It

---

*Private delivery services. In Philadelphia, messenger boys were employed by the American District Telegraph Company. The messenger boys were low paid and ill treated, generally ignored by the unions organizing for higher wages. They regularly worked long hours (before child labor laws restricted them) in conditions described as "vice and crime" by one writer (Philip Davis, "The Night Messenger Boy," *Boston Evening Transcript*, March 11, 1911).

was Gallegher who rang the alarm when the Woolwich Mills caught fire,* while the officer on the beat was asleep, and it was Gallegher who led the "Black Diamonds" against the "Wharf Rats," when they used to stone each other to their hearts' content on the coal-wharves of Richmond.†

I am afraid, now that I see these facts written down, that Gallegher was not a reputable character; but he was so very young and so very old for his years that we all liked him very much nevertheless. He lived in the extreme northern part of Philadelphia, where the cotton- and woollen-mills run down to the river, and how he ever got home after leaving the *Press*‡ building at two in the morning, was one of the mysteries of the office. Sometimes he caught a night car, and sometimes he walked all the way, arriving at the little house, where his mother and himself lived alone, at four in the morning. Occasionally he was given a ride on an early milk-cart, or on one of the newspaper delivery wagons, with its high piles of papers still damp and sticky from the press. He knew several drivers of "night hawks"—those cabs that prowl the streets at night looking for belated passengers— and when it was a very cold morning he would not go home at all, but would crawl into one of these cabs and sleep, curled up on the cushions, until daylight.

Besides being quick and cheerful, Gallegher possessed a power of amusing the *Press*'s young men to a degree seldom attained by the ordinary mortal. His clog-dancing§ on the city

---

*This appears to be a fictional fire.

---

†A district of Philadelphia, just south of the modern Betsy Ross Bridge, it was a major terminus for coal transported from the Reading Railroad facility. The names referenced are fictional gangs that operated in the area.

---

‡The *Philadelphia Press* was published from 1857 to 1920. Richard Harding Davis was a reporter there from 1886 to 1889.

---

§A step dance wearing inflexible wooden-soled shoes. Did Gallegher keep a pair at the office just for this purpose?

editor's desk, when that gentleman was upstairs fighting for two more columns of space, was always a source of innocent joy to us, and his imitations of the comedians of the variety halls delighted even the dramatic critic, from whom the comedians themselves failed to force a smile.

But Gallegher's chief characteristic was his love for that element of news generically classed as "crime." Not that he ever did anything criminal himself. On the contrary, his was rather the work of the criminal specialist, and his morbid interest in the doings of all queer characters, his knowledge of their methods, their present whereabouts, and their past deeds of transgression often rendered him a valuable ally to our police reporter, whose daily feuilletons* were the only portion of the paper Gallegher deigned to read.

In Gallegher the detective element was abnormally developed. He had shown this on several occasions, and to excellent purpose.

Once the paper had sent him into a Home for Destitute Orphans which was believed to be grievously mismanaged, and Gallegher, while playing the part of a destitute orphan, kept his eyes open to what was going on around him so faithfully that the story he told of the treatment meted out to the real orphans was sufficient to rescue the unhappy little wretches from the individual who had them in charge, and to have the individual himself sent to jail.

Gallegher's knowledge of the aliases, terms of imprisonment, and various misdoings of the leading criminals in Philadelphia was almost as thorough as that of the chief of police himself, and he could tell to an hour when "Dutchy Mack" was to be let out of prison, and could identify at a glance "Dick Oxford, confidence man," as "Gentleman Dan, petty thief."

---

*A section of the newspaper devoted to fiction or criticism, the purpose of which was to entertain the reader. Why would the police reporter's reportage be in this section?

There were, at this time, only two pieces of news in any of the papers. The least important of the two was the big fight between the Champion of the United States and the Would-be Champion,[*] arranged to take place near Philadelphia; the second was the Burrbank murder, which was filling space in newspapers all over the world, from New York to Bombay.

Richard F. Burrbank[†] was one of the most prominent of New York's railroad lawyers; he was also, as a matter of course, an owner of much railroad stock, and a very wealthy man. He had been spoken of as a political possibility for many high offices, and, as the counsel for a great railroad, was known even further than the great railroad itself had stretched its system.

At six o'clock one morning he was found by his butler lying at the foot of the hall stairs with two pistol wounds above his heart. He was quite dead. His safe, to which only he and his secretary had the keys, was found open, and $200,000[‡] in bonds, stocks, and money, which had been placed there only the night before, was found missing. The secretary was missing also. His name was Stephen S. Hade, and his name and his description had been telegraphed and cabled to all parts of the world. There was enough circumstantial evidence to show, beyond any question or possibility of mistake, that he was the murderer.

---

[*]The Champion of the United States might have been the Boston-born John L. Sullivan, reigning de facto from 1882 to 1892. In a monumental fight with Jake Kilrain on July 8, 1889, Sullivan won, retaining the heavyweight bare-knuckle title and receiving, for the first time, a title as heavyweight champion of the world. The fight was notable as the first American title fight using the London Prize Ring Rules. The fight was not "near Philadelphia," however; it was held in Richburg, Mississippi, over one thousand miles away. Another candidate for the unnamed Champion is the Irish American Jack McAuliffe, who held the title of world lightweight champion from 1866 to 1893. McAuliffe fought Mike Daly to a draw at the Cribb Club in Boston on December 5, 1889, "near Philadelphia." McAuliffe retired in 1897, undefeated.

[†]A fictional character with no known basis.

[‡]The equivalent of at least $6 million in 2023. Williamson, Measuring Worth, 2023.

It made an enormous amount of talk, and unhappy individuals were being arrested all over the country, and sent on to New York for identification. Three had been arrested at Liverpool, and one man just as he landed at Sydney, Australia. But so far the murderer had escaped.

We were all talking about it one night, as everybody else was all over the country, in the local room, and the city editor said it was worth a fortune to any one who chanced to run across Hade and succeeded in handing him over to the police. Some of us thought Hade had taken passage from some one of the smaller seaports, and others were of the opinion that he had buried himself in some cheap lodging-house in New York, or in one of the smaller towns in New Jersey.

"I shouldn't be surprised to meet him out walking, right here in Philadelphia," said one of the staff. "He'll be disguised, of course, but you could always tell him by the absence of the trigger finger on his right hand. It's missing, you know; shot off when he was a boy."

"You want to look for a man dressed like a tough," said the city editor; "for as this fellow is to all appearances a gentleman, he will try to look as little like a gentleman as possible."

"No, he won't," said Gallegher, with that calm impertinence that made him dear to us. "He'll dress just like a gentleman. Toughs don't wear gloves, and you see he's got to wear 'em. The first thing he thought of after doing for Burrbank was of that gone finger, and how he was to hide it. He stuffed the finger of that glove with cotton so's to make it look like a whole finger, and the first time he takes off that glove they've got him—see, and he knows it. So what youse want to do is to look for a man with gloves on. I've been a-doing it for two weeks now, and I can tell you it's hard work, for everybody wears gloves this kind of weather. But if you look long enough you'll find him. And when you think it's him, go up to him and hold out your hand in a friendly way, like a bunco-steerer, and shake his hand; and if you feel that his forefinger ain't real flesh, but just wadded cotton, then grip to it with your right and grab his throat with your left, and holler for help."

There was an appreciative pause.

"I see, gentlemen," said the city editor, dryly, "that Gallegher's reasoning has impressed you; and I also see that before the week is out all of my young men will be under bonds for assaulting innocent pedestrians whose only offence is that they wear gloves in midwinter."

———————

It was about a week after this that Detective Hefflefinger, of Inspector Byrnes's staff, came over to Philadelphia after a burglar, of whose whereabouts he had been misinformed by telegraph. He brought the warrant, requisition, and other necessary papers with him, but the burglar had flown. One of our reporters had worked on a New York paper, and knew Hefflefinger, and the detective came to the office to see if he could help him in his so far unsuccessful search.

He gave Gallegher his card, and after Gallegher had read it, and had discovered who the visitor was, he became so demoralized that he was absolutely useless.

"One of Byrnes's men"* was a much more awe-inspiring individual to Gallegher than a member of the Cabinet. He

---

*Thomas F. Byrnes (1842–1910) was the near-legendary chief of detectives of the New York Police Department between 1880 and 1895. In 1886, he published *Professional Criminals of America* and popularized the idea of databases of photographs of criminals. Though he is credited with inventing the modern police detective bureau, Byrnes was also renowned for his use of the "third degree" in extracting confessions. As a result, he undoubtedly convicted many innocents. He was forced to resign in 1895 by Police Commissioner Theodore Roosevelt, who had pledged to rid the department of corruption.

accordingly seized his hat and overcoat, and leaving his duties to be looked after by others, hastened out after the object of his admiration, who found his suggestions and knowledge of the city so valuable, and his company so entertaining, that they became very intimate, and spent the rest of the day together.

In the meanwhile the managing editor had instructed his subordinates to inform Gallegher, when he condescended to return, that his services were no longer needed. Gallegher had played truant once too often. Unconscious of this, he remained with his new friend until late the same evening, and started the next afternoon toward the *Press* office.

As I have said, Gallegher lived in the most distant part of the city, not many minutes' walk from the Kensington railroad station, where trains ran into the suburbs and on to New York.

It was in front of this station that a smoothly shaven, well-dressed man brushed past Gallegher and hurried up the steps to the ticket office.

He held a walking-stick in his right hand, and Gallegher, who now patiently scrutinized the hands of every one who wore gloves, saw that while three fingers of the man's hand were closed around the cane, the fourth stood out in almost a straight line with his palm.

Gallegher stopped with a gasp and with a trembling all over his little body, and his brain asked with a throb if it could be possible. But possibilities and probabilities were to be discovered later. Now was the time for action.

He was after the man in a moment, hanging at his heels and his eyes moist with excitement. He heard the man ask for a ticket to Torresdale, a little station just outside of Philadelphia, and when he was out of hearing, but not out of sight, purchased one for the same place.

The stranger went into the smoking-car, and seated himself at one end toward the door. Gallegher took his place at the opposite end.

He was trembling all over, and suffered from a slight feeling of nausea. He guessed it came from fright, not of any bodily harm that might come to him, but at the probability of failure in his adventure and of its most momentous possibilities.

The stranger pulled his coat collar up around his ears, hiding the lower portion of his face, but not concealing the resemblance in his troubled eyes and close-shut lips to the likenesses of the murderer Hade.

They reached Torresdale in half an hour, and the stranger, alighting quickly, struck off at a rapid pace down the country road leading to the station.

Gallegher gave him a hundred yards' start, and then followed slowly after. The road ran between fields and past a few frame-houses set far from the road in kitchen gardens.

Once or twice the man looked back over his shoulder, but he saw only a dreary length of road with a small boy splashing through the slush in the midst of it and stopping every now and again to throw snowballs at belated sparrows.

After a ten minutes' walk the stranger turned into a side road which led to only one place, the Eagle Inn, an old roadside hostelry known now as the headquarters for pothunters* from the Philadelphia game market and the battle-ground of many a cock-fight.

Gallegher knew the place well. He and his young companions had often stopped there when out chestnutting on holidays in the autumn.

The son of the man who kept it had often accompanied them on their excursions, and though the boys of the

---

*Those who kill for food rather than for sport.

city streets considered him a dumb lout, they respected him somewhat owing to his inside knowledge of dog- and cock-fights.

The stranger entered the inn at a side door, and Gallegher, reaching it a few minutes later, let him go for the time being, and set about finding his occasional playmate, young Keppler.

Keppler's offspring was found in the wood-shed.

"'Tain't hard to guess what brings you out here," said the tavern-keeper's son, with a grin; "it's the fight."

"What fight?" asked Gallegher, unguardedly.

"What fight? Why, *the* fight," returned his companion, with the slow contempt of superior knowledge. "It's to come off here to-night. You knew that as well as me; anyway your sportin' editor knows it. He got the tip last night, but that won't help you any. You needn't think there's any chance of your getting a peep at it. Why, tickets is two hundred and fifty apiece!'"

"Whew!" whistled Gallegher, "where's it to be?"

"In the barn," whispered Keppler. "I helped 'em fix the ropes this morning, I did."

"Gosh, but you're in luck," exclaimed Gallegher, with flattering envy. "Couldn't I jest get a peep at it?"

"Maybe," said the gratified Keppler. "There's a winder with

---

*Prizefighting was clearly illegal in Pennsylvania. Not only were the fighters guilty of misdemeanors, but also "anyone being present at such a fight, or laying any bet or wager on the result thereof, whether present or not" was considered a participant in the illegality (Laws of the General Assembly of the Commonwealth of Pennsylvania [enacted March 22, 1867], No. 22: 39). There was a loophole, however: "In 1883, the Pennsylvania courts upheld the city solicitor of Philadelphia by indicating that 'sparring exhibitions were not forbidden nor were they unlawful…and whether they were likely to be conducted as to cause a breach of the peace, was a matter for the mayor [of a given locality] to decide.' Thus, if a promoter of a 'sparring exhibition' could win the approval of a mayor, the fight was on." Thomas M. Croak, "The Professionalization of Prizefighting: Pittsburgh at the Turn of the Century," *Western Pennsylvania History* (1979): 333–43, quote from 336. The contests were immensely popular in ethnic, working-class neighborhoods and towns.

a wooden shutter at the back of the barn. You can get in by it, if you have some one to boost you up to the sill."

"Sa-a-y," drawled Gallegher, as if something had but just that moment reminded him. "Who's that gent who come down the road just a bit ahead of me—him with the cape-coat! Has he got anything to do with the fight?"

"Him?" repeated Keppler in tones of sincere disgust. "No-oh, he ain't no sport. He's queer, Dad thinks. He come here one day last week about ten in the morning, said his doctor told him to go out 'en the country for his health. He's stuck up and citified, and wears gloves, and takes his meals private in his room, and all that sort of ruck. They was saying in the saloon last night that they thought he was hiding from something, and Dad, just to try him, asks him last night if he was coming to see the fight. He looked sort of scared, and said he didn't want to see no fight. And then Dad says, 'I guess you mean you don't want no fighters to see you.' Dad didn't mean no harm by it, just passed it as a joke; but Mr. Carleton, as he calls himself, got white as a ghost an' says, 'I'll go to the fight willing enough,' and begins to laugh and joke. And this morning he went right into the bar-room, where all the sports were setting, and said he was going into town to see some friends; and as he starts off he laughs an' says, 'This don't look as if I was afraid of seeing people, does it?' but Dad says it was just bluff that made him do it, and Dad thinks that if he hadn't said what he did, this Mr. Carleton wouldn't have left his room at all."

Gallegher had got all he wanted, and much more than he had hoped for—so much more that his walk back to the station was in the nature of a triumphal march.

He had twenty minutes to wait for the next train, and it seemed an hour. While waiting he sent a telegram to Hefflefinger at his hotel. It read: "Your man is near the Torresdale station, on

Pennsylvania Railroad; take cab, and meet me at station. Wait until I come. GALLEGHER."

With the exception of one at midnight, no other train stopped at Torresdale that evening, hence the direction to take a cab.

The train to the city seemed to Gallegher to drag itself by inches. It stopped and backed at purposeless intervals, waited for an express to precede it, and dallied at stations, and when, at last, it reached the terminus, Gallegher was out before it had stopped and was in the cab and off on his way to the home of the sporting editor.

The sporting editor was at dinner and came out in the hall to see him, with his napkin in his hand. Gallegher explained breathlessly that he had located the murderer for whom the police of two continents were looking, and that he believed, in order to quiet the suspicions of the people with whom he was hiding, that he would be present at the fight that night.

The sporting editor led Gallegher into his library and shut the door. "Now," he said, "go over all that again."

Gallegher went over it again in detail, and added how he had sent for Hefflefinger to make the arrest in order that it might be kept from the knowledge of the local police and from the Philadelphia reporters.

"What I want Hefflefinger to do is to arrest Hade with the warrant he has for the burglar," explained Gallegher; "and to take him on to New York on the owl train that passes Torresdale at one. It don't get to Jersey City until four o'clock, one hour after the morning papers go to press. Of course, we must fix Hefflefinger so's he'll keep quiet and not tell who his prisoner really is."

The sporting editor reached his hand out to pat Gallegher on the head, but changed his mind and shook hands with him instead.

"My boy," he said, "you are an infant phenomenon. If I can pull the rest of this thing off to-night it will mean the $5,000 reward and fame galore for you and the paper. Now, I'm going to write a note to the managing editor, and you can take it around to him and tell him what you've done and what I am going to do, and he'll take you back on the paper and raise your salary. Perhaps you didn't know you've been discharged?"

"Do you think you ain't a-going to take me with you?" demanded Gallegher.

"Why, certainly not. Why should I? It all lies with the detective and myself now. You've done your share, and done it well. If the man's caught, the reward's yours. But you'd only be in the way now. You'd better go to the office and make your peace with the chief."

"If the paper can get along without me, I can get along without the old paper," said Gallegher, hotly. "And if I ain't a-going with you, you ain't neither, for I know where Hefflefinger is to be, and you don't, and I won't tell you."

"Oh, very well, very well," replied the sporting editor, weakly capitulating. "I'll send the note by a messenger; only mind, if you lose your place, don't blame me."

Gallegher wondered how this man could value a week's salary against the excitement of seeing a noted criminal run down, and of getting the news to the paper, and to that one paper alone.

From that moment the sporting editor sank in Gallegher's estimation.

Mr. Dwyer sat down at his desk and scribbled off the following note:

"I have received reliable information that Hade, the Burrbank murderer, will be present at the fight to-night. We have arranged it so that he will be arrested quietly and

*in such a manner that the fact may be kept from all other
papers. I need not point out to you that this will be the most
important piece of news in the country to-morrow.*

"*Yours, etc.,*

MICHAEL E. DWYER."

The sporting editor stepped into the waiting cab, while
Gallegher whispered the directions to the driver. He was told to
go first to a district-messenger office, and from there up to the
Ridge Avenue Road, out Broad Street, and on to the old Eagle
Inn, near Torresdale.

It was a miserable night. The rain and snow were falling together,
and freezing as they fell. The sporting editor got out to send his
message to the *Press* office, and then lighting a cigar, and turning
up the collar of his great-coat, curled up in the corner of the cab.

"Wake me when we get there, Gallegher," he said. He knew
he had a long ride, and much rapid work before him, and he was
preparing for the strain.

To Gallegher the idea of going to sleep seemed almost criminal. From the dark corner of the cab his eyes shone with excitement, and with the awful joy of anticipation. He glanced every
now and then to where the sporting editor's cigar shone in the
darkness, and watched it as it gradually burnt more dimly and
went out. The lights in the shop windows threw a broad glare
across the ice on the pavements, and the lights from the lamp-
posts tossed the distorted shadow of the cab, and the horse, and
the motionless driver, sometimes before and sometimes behind
them.

After half an hour Gallegher slipped down to the bottom of

the cab and dragged out a lap-robe, in which he wrapped himself. It was growing colder, and the damp, keen wind swept in through the cracks until the window-frames and woodwork were cold to the touch.

An hour passed, and the cab was still moving more slowly over the rough surface of partly paved streets, and by single rows of new houses standing at different angles to each other in fields covered with ash-heaps and brick-kilns. Here and there the gaudy lights of a drug-store, and the forerunner of suburban civilization, shone from the end of a new block of houses, and the rubber cape of an occasional policeman showed in the light of the lamp-post that he hugged for comfort.

Then even the houses disappeared, and the cab dragged its way between truck farms, with desolate-looking glass-covered beds, and pools of water, half-caked with ice, and bare trees, and interminable fences.

Once or twice the cab stopped altogether, and Gallegher could hear the driver swearing to himself, or at the horse, or the roads. At last they drew up before the station at Torresdale. It was quite deserted, and only a single light cut a swath in the darkness and showed a portion of the platform, the ties, and the rails glistening in the rain. They walked twice past the light before a figure stepped out of the shadow and greeted them cautiously.

"I am Mr. Dwyer, of the *Press*," said the sporting editor, briskly. "You've heard of me, perhaps. Well, there shouldn't be any difficulty in our making a deal, should there? This boy here has found Hade, and we have reason to believe he will be among the spectators at the fight to-night. We want you to arrest him quietly, and as secretly as possible. You can do it with your papers and your badge easily enough. We want you to pretend that you believe he is this burglar you came over after. If you will

do this, and take him away without any one so much as suspect-
ing who he really is, and on the train that passes here at 1.20 for
New York, we will give you $500 out of the $5,000 reward. If,
however, one other paper, either in New York or Philadelphia,
or anywhere else, knows of the arrest, you won't get a cent. Now,
what do you say?"

The detective had a great deal to say. He wasn't at all sure
the man Gallegher suspected was Hade; he feared he might get
himself into trouble by making a false arrest, and if it should be
the man, he was afraid the local police would interfere.

"We've no time to argue or debate this matter," said Dwyer,
warmly. "We agree to point Hade out to you in the crowd. After
the fight is over you arrest him as we have directed, and you get
the money and the credit of the arrest. If you don't like this, I
will arrest the man myself, and have him driven to town, with a
pistol for a warrant."

Hefflefinger considered in silence and then agreed uncondi-
tionally. "As you say, Mr. Dwyer," he returned. "I've heard of you
for a thoroughbred sport. I know you'll do what you say you'll
do; and as for me I'll do what you say and just as you say, and it's
a very pretty piece of work as it stands."

They all stepped back into the cab, and then it was that they
were met by a fresh difficulty, how to get the detective into the
barn where the fight was to take place, for neither of the two
men had $250 to pay for his admittance.

But this was overcome when Gallegher remembered the
window of which young Keppler had told him.

In the event of Hade's losing courage and not daring to show
himself in the crowd around the ring, it was agreed that Dwyer
should come to the barn and warn Hefflefinger; but if he should
come, Dwyer was merely to keep near him and to signify by a
prearranged gesture which one of the crowd he was.

They drew up before a great black shadow of a house, dark, forbidding, and apparently deserted. But at the sound of the wheels on the gravel the door opened, letting out a stream of warm, cheerful light, and a man's voice said, "Put out those lights. Don't youse know no better than that?" This was Keppler, and he welcomed Mr. Dwyer with effusive courtesy.

The two men showed in the stream of light, and the door closed on them, leaving the house as it was at first, black and silent, save for the dripping of the rain and snow from the eaves.

The detective and Gallegher put out the cab's lamps and led the horse toward a long, low shed in the rear of the yard, which they now noticed was almost filled with teams of many different makes, from the Hobson's choice of a livery stable* to the brougham of the man about town.

"No," said Gallegher, as the cabman stopped to hitch the horse beside the others, "we want it nearest that lower gate. When we newspaper men leave this place we'll leave it in a hurry, and the man who is nearest town is likely to get there first. You won't be a-following of no hearse when you make your return trip."

Gallegher tied the horse to the very gate-post itself, leaving the gate open and allowing a clear road and a flying start for the prospective race to Newspaper Row.

The driver disappeared under the shelter of the porch, and Gallegher and the detective moved off cautiously to the rear of the barn. "This must be the window," said Hefflefinger, pointing to a broad wooden shutter some feet from the ground.

---

*Tobias Hobson was a carrier and innkeeper at Cambridge. According to an account in *The Spectator* (509, Oct. 10, 1712), "[Hobson] kept a stable of forty good cattle, always ready and fit for travelling; but when a man came for a horse he was led into the stable, where there was great choice, but was obliged to take the horse which stood nearest to the stable-door; so that every customer was alike well served, according to his chance, and every horse ridden with the same justice. From whence it became a proverb, when what ought to be your election was forced upon you, to say, *Hobson's Choice*."

"Just you give me a boost once, and I'll get that open in a jiffy," said Gallegher.

The detective placed his hands on his knees, and Gallegher stood upon his shoulders, and with the blade of his knife lifted the wooden button that fastened the window on the inside, and pulled the shutter open.

Then he put one leg inside over the sill, and leaning down helped to draw his fellow-conspirator up to a level with the window. "I feel just like I was burglarizing a house," chuckled Gallegher, as he dropped noiselessly to the floor below and refastened the shutter. The barn was a large one, with a row of stalls on either side in which horses and cows were dozing. There was a hay-mow over each row of stalls, and at one end of the barn a number of fence-rails had been thrown across from one mow to the other. These rails were covered with hay.

In the middle of the floor was the ring. It was not really a ring, but a square, with wooden posts at its four corners through which ran a heavy rope. The space inclosed by the rope was covered with sawdust.

Gallegher could not resist stepping into the ring, and after stamping the sawdust once or twice, as if to assure himself that he was really there, began dancing around it, and indulging in such a remarkable series of fistic manœuvres with an imaginary adversary that the unimaginative detective precipitately backed into a corner of the barn.

"Now, then," said Gallegher, having apparently vanquished his foe, "you come with me." His companion followed quickly as Gallegher climbed to one of the hay-mows, and crawling carefully out on the fence-rail, stretched himself at full length, face downward. In this position, by moving the straw a little, he could look down, without being himself seen, upon the heads of whomsoever stood below. "This is better'n a private box, ain't it?" said Gallegher.

Gallegher stood upon his shoulders.

The boy from the newspaper office and the detective lay there in silence, biting at straws and tossing anxiously on their comfortable bed.

It seemed fully two hours before they came. Gallegher had listened without breathing, and with every muscle on a strain, at least a dozen times, when some movement in the yard had led him to believe that they were at the door. And he had numerous doubts and fears. Sometimes it was that the police had learnt of the fight, and had raided Keppler's in his absence, and again it was that the fight had been postponed, or, worst of all, that it would be put off until so late that Mr. Dwyer could not get back in time for the last edition of the paper. Their coming, when at last they came, was heralded by an advance-guard of two sporting men, who stationed themselves at either side of the big door.

"Hurry up, now, gents," one of the men said with a shiver, "don't keep this door open no longer'n is needful."

It was not a very large crowd, but it was wonderfully well selected. It ran, in the majority of its component parts, to heavy white coats with pearl buttons. The white coats were shouldered by long blue coats with astrakhan fur* trimmings, the wearers of which preserved a cliqueness not remarkable when one considers that they believed every one else present to be either a crook or a prize-fighter.

There were well-fed, well-groomed club-men and brokers in the crowd, a politician or two, a popular comedian with his manager, amateur boxers from the athletic clubs, and quiet, close-mouthed sporting men from every city in the country. Their names if printed in the papers would have been as familiar as the types of the papers themselves.

And among these men, whose only thought was of the brutal sport to come, was Hade, with Dwyer standing at ease at his shoulder,—Hade, white, and visibly in deep anxiety, hiding his pale face beneath a cloth travelling-cap, and with his chin muffled in a woollen scarf. He had dared to come because he feared his danger from the already suspicious Keppler was less than if he stayed away. And so he was there, hovering restlessly on the border of the crowd, feeling his danger and sick with fear.

When Hefflefinger first saw him he started up on his hands and elbows and made a movement forward as if he would leap down then and there and carry off his prisoner single-handed.

"Lie down," growled Gallegher; "an officer of any sort wouldn't live three minutes in that crowd."

---

*Dark curly fleece shorn from young karakul lambs bred in central Asia, popular as a trim for coats.

The detective drew back slowly and buried himself again in the straw, but never once through the long fight which followed did his eyes leave the person of the murderer. The newspaper men took their places in the foremost row close around the ring, and kept looking at their watches and begging the master of ceremonies to "shake it up, do."

There was a great deal of betting, and all of the men handled the great roll of bills they wagered with a flippant recklessness which could only be accounted for in Gallegher's mind by temporary mental derangement. Some one pulled a box out into the ring and the master of ceremonies mounted it, and pointed out in forcible language that as they were almost all already under bonds to keep the peace, it behooved all to curb their excitement and to maintain a severe silence, unless they wanted to bring the police upon them and have themselves "sent down" for a year or two.

Then two very disreputable-looking persons tossed their respective principals' high hats into the ring, and the crowd, recognizing in this relic of the days when brave knights threw down their gauntlets in the lists as only a sign that the fight was about to begin, cheered tumultuously.

This was followed by a sudden surging forward, and a mutter of admiration much more flattering than the cheers had been, when the principals followed their hats, and slipping out of their greatcoats, stood forth in all the physical beauty of the perfect brute.

Their pink skin was as soft and healthy looking as a baby's, and glowed in the lights of the lanterns like tinted ivory, and underneath this silken covering the great biceps and muscles moved in and out and looked like the coils of a snake around the branch of a tree.

Gentleman and blackguard shouldered each other for a nearer view; the coachmen, whose metal buttons were unpleasantly suggestive of police, put their hands, in the excitement of the moment, on the shoulders of their masters; the perspiration stood out in great drops on the foreheads of the backers, and the newspaper men bit somewhat nervously at the ends of their pencils.

And in the stalls the cows munched contentedly at their cuds and gazed with gentle curiosity at their two fellow-brutes, who stood waiting the signal to fall upon, and kill each other if need be, for the delectation of their brothers.

"Take your places," commanded the master of ceremonies.

In the moment in which the two men faced each other the crowd became so still that, save for the beating of the rain upon the shingled roof and the stamping of a horse in one of the stalls, the place was as silent as a church.

"Time," shouted the master of ceremonies.

The two men sprang into a posture of defence, which was lost as quickly as it was taken, one great arm shot out like a piston-rod; there was the sound of bare fists beating on naked flesh; there was an exultant indrawn gasp of savage pleasure and relief from the crowd, and the great fight had begun.

How the fortunes of war rose and fell, and changed and rechanged that night, is an old story to those who listen to such stories; and those who do not will be glad to be spared the telling of it. It was, they say, one of the bitterest fights between two men that this country has ever known.

But all that is of interest here is that after an hour of this desperate brutal business the champion ceased to be the favorite; the man whom he had taunted and bullied, and for whom the public had but little sympathy, was proving himself a likely winner, and under his cruel blows, as sharp and clean as those from a cutlass, his opponent was rapidly giving way.

The men about the ropes were past all control now; they drowned Keppler's petitions for silence with oaths and in inarticulate shouts of anger, as if the blows had fallen upon them, and in mad rejoicings. They swept from one end of the ring to the other, with every muscle leaping in unison with those of the man they favored, and when a New York correspondent muttered over his shoulder that this would be the biggest sporting surprise since the Heenan-Sayers fight,* Mr. Dwyer nodded his head sympathetically in assent.

In the excitement and tumult it is doubtful if any heard the three quickly repeated blows that fell heavily from the outside upon the big doors of the barn. If they did, it was already too late to mend matters, for the door fell, torn from its hinges, and as it fell a captain of police sprang into the light from out of the storm, with his lieutenants and their men crowding close at his shoulder.

In the panic and stampede that followed, several of the men stood as helplessly immovable as though they had seen a ghost; others made a mad rush into the arms of the officers and were beaten back against the ropes of the ring; others dived headlong into the stalls, among the horses and cattle, and still others shoved the rolls of money they held into the hands of the police and begged like children to be allowed to escape.

The instant the door fell and the raid was declared Hefflefinger slipped over the cross rails on which he had been lying, hung for an instant by his hands, and then dropped into the centre of the fighting mob on the floor. He was out of it in an instant with the agility of a pickpocket, was across the room and at Hade's throat like a dog. The murderer, for the moment, was the calmer man of the two.

---

*On April 17, 1860, the twenty-five-year-old John Carmel Heenan, a six-foot, two-inch American who weighed in at 195 pounds, took on "Brighton Titch" Tom Sayers, then thirty-four years old, five feet, eight inches in height and 149 pounds, in what was billed as the first international title match, in a field near Farnborough, Hampshire, England. The prize was four hundred pounds. They fought for forty-two rounds, lasting two and three-quarter hours, to a draw, the fight ending only when it was broken up by the Aldershot police. In attendance at the prizefight were Charles Dickens, William Makepeace Thackeray, the prime minister Lord Palmerston, and the nineteen-year-old Prince of Wales.

"Here," he panted, "hands off, now. There's no need for all this violence. There's no great harm in looking at a fight, is there? There's a hundred-dollar bill in my right hand; take it and let me slip out of this. No one is looking. Here."

But the detective only held him the closer.

"I want you for burglary," he whispered under his breath. "You've got to come with me now, and quick. The less fuss you make, the better for both of us. If you don't know who I am, you can feel my badge under my coat there. I've got the authority. It's all regular, and when we're out of this d—d row I'll show you the papers."

He took one hand from Hade's throat and pulled a pair of handcuffs from his pocket.

"It's a mistake. This is an outrage," gasped the murderer, white and trembling, but dreadfully alive and desperate for his liberty. "Let me go, I tell you! Take your hands off of me! Do I look like a burglar, you fool?"

"I know who you look like," whispered the detective, with his face close to the face of his prisoner. "Now, will you go easy as a burglar, or shall I tell these men who you are and what I *do* want you for? Shall I call out your real name or not? Shall I tell them? Quick, speak up; shall I?"

There was something so exultant—something so unnecessarily savage in the officer's face that the man he held saw that the detective knew him for what he really was, and the hands that had held his throat slipped down around his shoulders, or he would have fallen. The man's eyes opened and closed again, and he swayed weakly backward and forward, and choked as if his throat were dry and burning. Even to such a hardened connoisseur in crime as Gallegher, who stood closely by, drinking it in, there was something so abject in the man's terror that he regarded him with what was almost a touch of pity.

"For God's sake," Hade begged, "let me go. Come with me

to my room and I'll give you half the money. I'll divide with you fairly. We can both get away. There's a fortune for both of us there. We both can get away. You'll be rich for life. Do you understand—for life!"

But the detective, to his credit, only shut his lips the tighter.

"That's enough," he whispered, in return. "That's more than I expected. You've sentenced yourself already. Come!"

Two officers in uniform barred their exit at the door, but Hefflefinger smiled easily and showed his badge.

"One of Byrnes's men," he said, in explanation; "came over expressly to take this chap. He's a burglar; 'Arlie' Lane, *alias* Carleton. I've shown the papers to the captain. It's all regular. I'm just going to get his traps at the hotel and walk him over to the station. I guess we'll push right on to New York to-night."

The officers nodded and smiled their admiration for the representative of what is, perhaps, the best detective force in the world, and let him pass.

Then Hefflefinger turned and spoke to Gallegher, who still stood as watchful as a dog at his side. "I'm going to his room to get the bonds and stuff," he whispered; "then I'll march him to the station and take that train. I've done my share; don't forget yours!"

"Oh, you'll get your money right enough," said Gallegher. "And, sa-ay," he added, with the appreciative nod of an expert, "do you know, you did it rather well."

Mr. Dwyer had been writing while the raid was settling down, as he had been writing while waiting for the fight to begin. Now he walked over to where the other correspondents stood in angry conclave.

The newspaper men had informed the officers who hemmed them in that they represented the principal papers of the country, and were expostulating vigorously with the captain, who had planned the raid, and who declared they were under arrest.

"Don't be an ass, Scott," said Mr. Dwyer, who was too excited to be polite or politic. "You know our being here isn't a matter of choice. We came here on business, as you did, and you've no right to hold us."

"If we don't get our stuff on the wire at once," protested a New York man, "we'll be too late for to-morrow's paper, and———"

Captain Scott said he did not care a profanely small amount for to-morrow's paper, and that all he knew was that to the station-house the newspaper men would go. There they would have a hearing, and if the magistrate chose to let them off, that was the magistrate's business, but that his duty was to take them into custody.

"But then it will be too late, don't you understand?" shouted Mr. Dwyer. "You've got to let us go *now*, at once."

"For God's sake," Hade begged, "let me go!"

"I can't do it, Mr. Dwyer," said the captain, "and that's all there is to it. Why, haven't I just sent the president of the Junior Republican Club to the patrol-wagon, the man that put this coat on me, and do you think I can let you fellows go after that? You were all put under bonds to keep the peace not three days ago, and here you're at it—fighting like badgers. It's worth my place to let one of you off."

What Mr. Dwyer said next was so uncomplimentary to the gallant Captain Scott that that overwrought individual seized the sporting editor by the shoulder, and shoved him into the hands of two of his men.

This was more than the distinguished Mr. Dwyer could brook, and he excitedly raised his hand in resistance. But before he had time to do anything foolish his wrist was gripped by one strong, little hand, and he was conscious that another was picking the pocket of his great-coat.

He slapped his hands to his sides, and looking down, saw Gallegher standing close behind him and holding him by the wrist. Mr. Dwyer had forgotten the boy's existence, and would have spoken sharply if something in Gallegher's innocent eyes had not stopped him.

Gallegher's hand was still in that pocket, in which Mr. Dwyer had shoved his notebook filled with what he had written of Gallegher's work and Hade's final capture, and with a running descriptive account of the fight. With his eyes fixed on Mr. Dwyer, Gallegher drew it out, and with a quick movement shoved it inside his waistcoat. Mr. Dwyer gave a nod of comprehension. Then glancing at his two guardsmen, and finding that they were still interested in the wordy battle of the correspondents with their chief, and had seen nothing, he stooped and whispered to Gallegher: "The forms are locked at twenty minutes to three. If you don't get there by that time it will be of no use, but if you're on time you'll beat the town—and the country too."

Gallegher's eyes flashed significantly, and nodding his head to show he understood, started boldly on a run toward the door. But the officers who guarded it brought him to an abrupt halt, and, much to Mr. Dwyer's astonishment, drew from him what was apparently a torrent of tears.

"Let me go to me father. I want me father," the boy shrieked, hysterically. "They've 'rested father. Oh, daddy, daddy. They're a-goin' to take you to prison."

"Who is your father, sonny?" asked one of the guardians of the gate.

"Keppler's me father," sobbed Gallegher. "They're a-goin' to lock him up, and I'll never see him no more."

"Oh, yes, you will," said the officer, good-naturedly; "he's there in that first patrol-wagon. You can run over and say good night to him, and then you'd better get to bed. This ain't no place for kids of your age."

"Thank you, sir," sniffed Gallegher, tearfully, as the two officers raised their clubs, and let him pass out into the darkness.

The yard outside was in a tumult, horses were stamping, and plunging, and backing the carriages into one another; lights were flashing from every window of what had been apparently an uninhabited house, and the voices of the prisoners were still raised in angry expostulation.

Three police patrol-wagons were moving about the yard, filled with unwilling passengers, who sat or stood, packed together like sheep, and with no protection from the sleet and rain.

Gallegher stole off into a dark corner, and watched the scene until his eyesight became familiar with the position of the land.

Then with his eyes fixed fearfully on the swinging light of

a lantern with which an officer was searching among the carriages, he groped his way between horses' hoofs and behind the wheels of carriages to the cab which he had himself placed at the furthermost gate. It was still there, and the horse, as he had left it, with its head turned toward the city. Gallegher opened the big gate noiselessly, and worked nervously at the hitching strap. The knot was covered with a thin coating of ice, and it was several minutes before he could loosen it. But his teeth finally pulled it apart, and with the reins in his hands he sprang upon the wheel. And as he stood so, a shock of fear ran down his back like an electric current, his breath left him, and he stood immovable, gazing with wide eyes into the darkness.

The officer with the lantern had suddenly loomed up from behind a carriage not fifty feet distant, and was standing perfectly still, with his lantern held over his head, peering so directly toward Gallegher that the boy felt that he must see him. Gallegher stood with one foot on the hub of the wheel and with the other on the box waiting to spring. It seemed a minute before either of them moved, and then the officer took a step forward, and demanded sternly, "Who is that? What are you doing there?"

There was no time for parley then. Gallegher felt that he had been taken in the act, and that his only chance lay in open flight. He leaped up on the box, pulling out the whip as he did so, and with a quick sweep lashed the horse across the head and back. The animal sprang forward with a snort, narrowly clearing the gate-post, and plunged off into the darkness.

"Stop!" cried the officer.

So many of Gallegher's acquaintances among the longshoremen and mill hands had been challenged in so much the same manner that Gallegher knew what would probably follow if the challenge was disregarded. So he slipped from his seat to the footboard below, and ducked his head.

The three reports of a pistol, which rang out briskly from behind him, proved that his early training had given him a valuable fund of useful miscellaneous knowledge.

"Don't you be scared," he said, reassuringly, to the horse; "he's firing in the air."

The pistol-shots were answered by the impatient clangor of a patrol-wagon's gong, and glancing over his shoulder Gallegher saw its red and green lanterns tossing from side to side and looking in the darkness like the side-lights of a yacht plunging forward in a storm.

"I hadn't bargained to race you against no patrol-wagons," said Gallegher to his animal; "but if they want a race, we'll give them a tough tussle for it, won't we?"

Philadelphia, lying four miles to the south, sent up a faint yellow glow to the sky. It seemed very far away, and Gallegher's braggadocio grew cold within him at the loneliness of his adventure and the thought of the long ride before him.

It was still bitterly cold.

The rain and sleet beat through his clothes, and struck his skin with a sharp chilling touch that set him trembling.

Even the thought of the over-weighted patrol-wagon probably sticking in the mud some safe distance in the rear, failed to cheer him, and the excitement that had so far made him callous to the cold died out and left him weaker and nervous. But his horse was chilled with the long standing, and now leaped eagerly forward, only too willing to warm the half-frozen blood in its veins.

"You're a good beast," said Gallegher, plaintively. "You've got more nerve than me. Don't you go back on me now. Mr. Dwyer says we've got to beat the town." Gallegher had no idea what time it was as he rode through the night, but he knew he would be able to find out from a big clock over a manufactory at a point nearly three-quarters of the distance from Keppler's to the goal.

He was still in the open country and driving recklessly, for he knew the best part of his ride must be made outside the city limits.

He raced between desolate-looking corn-fields with bare stalks and patches of muddy earth rising above the thin covering of snow, truck farms and brick-yards fell behind him on either side. It was very lonely work, and once or twice the dogs ran yelping to the gates and barked after him.

Part of his way lay parallel with the railroad tracks, and he drove for some time beside long lines of freight and coal cars as they stood resting for the night. The fantastic Queen Anne suburban stations were dark and deserted, but in one or two of the block-towers he could see the operators writing at their desks, and the sight in some way comforted him.

Once he thought of stopping to get out the blanket in which he had wrapped himself on the first trip, but he feared to spare the time, and drove on with his teeth chattering and his shoulders shaking with the cold.

He welcomed the first solitary row of darkened houses with a faint cheer of recognition. The scattered lamp-posts lightened his spirits, and even the badly paved streets rang under the beats of his horse's feet like music. Great mills and manufactories, with only a night-watchman's light in the lowest of their many stories, began to take the place of the gloomy farm-houses and gaunt trees that had startled him with their grotesque shapes. He had been driving nearly an hour, he calculated, and in that time the rain had changed to a wet snow, that fell heavily and clung to whatever it touched. He passed block after block of trim workmen's houses, as still and silent as the sleepers within them, and at last he turned the horse's head into Broad Street, the city's great thoroughfare, that stretches from its one end to the other and cuts it evenly in two.

He was driving noiselessly over the snow and slush in the street, with his thoughts bent only on the clock-face he wished so much to see, when a hoarse voice challenged him from the sidewalk. "Hey, you, stop there, hold up!" said the voice.

Gallegher turned his head, and though he saw that the voice came from under a policeman's helmet, his only answer was to hit his horse sharply over the head with his whip and to urge it into a gallop.

This, on his part, was followed by a sharp, shrill whistle from the policeman. Another whistle answered it from a street-corner one block ahead of him. "Whoa," said Gallegher, pulling on the reins. "There's one too many of them," he added, in apologetic explanation. The horse stopped, and stood, breathing heavily, with great clouds of steam rising from its flanks.

"Why in hell didn't you stop when I told you to?" demanded the voice, now close at the cab's side.

"I didn't hear you," returned Gallegher, sweetly. "But I heard you whistle, and I heard your partner whistle, and I thought maybe it was me you wanted to speak to, so I just stopped."

"You heard me well enough. Why aren't your lights lit?" demanded the voice.

"Should I have 'em lit?" asked Gallegher, bending over and regarding them with sudden interest.

"You know you should, and if you don't, you've no right to be driving that cab. I don't believe you're the regular driver, anyway. Where'd you get it?"

"It ain't my cab, of course," said Gallegher, with an easy laugh. "It's Luke McGovern's. He left it outside Cronin's while he went in to get a drink, and he took too much, and me father told me to drive it round to the stable for him. I'm Cronin's son. McGovern ain't in no condition to drive. You can see yourself how he's been misusing the horse. He puts it up at Bachman's livery stable, and I was just going around there now."

Gallegher's knowledge of the local celebrities of the district confused the zealous officer of the peace. He surveyed the boy with a steady stare that would have distressed a less skilful liar, but Gallegher only shrugged his shoulders slightly, as if from the cold, and waited with apparent indifference to what the officer would say next.

In reality his heart was beating heavily against his side, and he felt that if he was kept on a strain much longer he would give way and break down. A second snow-covered form emerged suddenly from the shadow of the houses.

"What is it, Reeder?" it asked.

"Oh, nothing much," replied the first officer. "This kid hadn't any lamps lit, so I called to him to stop and he didn't do it, so I whistled to you. It's all right, though. He's just taking it round to Bachman's. Go ahead," he added, sulkily.

"Get up!" chirped Gallegher. "Good night," he added, over his shoulder.

Gallegher gave an hysterical little gasp of relief as he trotted away from the two policemen, and poured bitter maledictions on their heads for two meddling fools as he went.

"They might as well kill a man as scare him to death," he said, with an attempt to get back to his customary flippancy. But the effort was somewhat pitiful, and he felt guiltily conscious that a salt, warm tear was creeping slowly down his face, and that a lump that would not keep down was rising in his throat.

"'Tain't no fair thing for the whole police force to keep worrying at a little boy like me," he said, in shame-faced apology. "I'm not doing nothing wrong, and I'm half froze to death, and yet they keep a-nagging at me."

It was so cold that when the boy stamped his feet against the footboard to keep them warm, sharp pains shot up through his body, and when he beat his arms about his shoulders, as he had seen real cabmen do, the blood in his finger-tips tingled so acutely that he cried aloud with the pain.

He had often been up that late before, but he had never felt so sleepy. It was as if some one was pressing a sponge heavy with chloroform near his face, and he could not fight off the drowsiness that lay hold of him.

He saw, dimly hanging above his head, a round disc of light that seemed like a great moon, and which he finally guessed to be the clock-face for which he had been on the look-out. He had passed it before he realized this; but the fact stirred him into wakefulness again, and when his cab's wheels slipped around the City Hall corner, he remembered to look up at the other big clock-face that keeps awake over the railroad station and measures out the night.

He gave a gasp of consternation when he saw that it was half-past two, and that there was but ten minutes left to him. This, and the many electric lights and the sight of the familiar pile of buildings, startled him into a semi-consciousness of where he was and how great was the necessity for haste.

He rose in his seat and called on the horse, and urged it into a reckless gallop over the slippery asphalt. He considered nothing else but speed, and looking neither to the left nor right dashed off down Broad Street into Chestnut, where his course lay straight away to the office, now only seven blocks distant.

Gallegher never knew how it began, but he was suddenly assaulted by shouts on either side, his horse was thrown back on its haunches, and he found two men in cabmen's livery hanging at its head, and patting its sides, and calling it by name. And the other cabmen who have their stand at the corner were swarming about the carriage, all of them talking and swearing at once, and gesticulating wildly with their whips.

They said they knew the cab was McGovern's, and they wanted to know where he was, and why he wasn't on it; they wanted to know where Gallegher had stolen it, and why he had been such a fool as to drive it into the arms of its owner's friends; they said that it was about time that a cab-driver could get off his box to take a drink without having his cab run away with, and some of them called loudly for a policeman to take the young thief in charge.

Gallegher felt as if he had been suddenly dragged into consciousness out of a bad dream, and stood for a second like a half-awakened somnambulist.

They had stopped the cab under an electric light, and its glare shone coldly down upon the trampled snow and the faces of the men around him.

Gallegher bent forward, and lashed savagely at the horse with his whip.

"Let me go," he shouted, as he tugged impotently at the reins. "Let me go, I tell you. I haven't stole no cab, and you've got no right to stop me. I only want to take it to the *Press* office," he begged. "They'll send it back to you all right. They'll pay you for the trip. I'm not running away with it. The driver's got the collar—he's 'rested—and I'm only a-going to the *Press* office. Do you hear me?" he cried, his voice rising and breaking in a shriek of passion and disappointment. "I tell you to let go those reins. Let me go, or I'll kill you. Do you hear me? I'll kill you." And leaning forward, the boy struck savagely with his long whip at the faces of the men about the horse's head.

Some one in the crowd reached up and caught him by the ankles, and with a quick jerk pulled him off the box, and threw him on to the street. But he was up on his knees in a moment, and caught at the man's hand.

"Don't let them stop me, mister," he cried, "please let me go. I didn't steal the cab, sir. S'help me, I didn't. I'm telling you the truth. Take me to the *Press* office, and they'll prove it to you. They'll pay you anything you ask 'em. It's only such a little ways now, and I've come so far, sir. Please don't let them stop me," he sobbed, clasping the man about the knees. "For Heaven's sake, mister, let me go!"

———————

The managing editor of the *Press* took up the india-rubber speaking-tube* at his side, and answered, "Not yet" to an inquiry the night editor had already put to him five times within the last twenty minutes.

Then he snapped the metal top of the tube impatiently, and went upstairs. As he passed the door of the local room, he noticed that the reporters had not gone home, but were sitting about on the tables and chairs, waiting. They looked up inquiringly as he passed, and the city editor asked, "Any news yet?" and the managing editor shook his head.

The compositors were standing idle in the composing-room, and their foreman was talking with the night editor.

"Well," said that gentleman, tentatively.

"Well," returned the managing editor, "I don't think we can wait; do you?"

"It's a half-hour after time now," said the night editor, "and we'll miss the suburban trains if we hold the paper back any longer. We can't afford to wait for a purely hypothetical story. The chances are all against the fight's having taken place or this Hade's having been arrested."

———————

*A primitive intercom, consisting of two cones connected by an air pipe (here India rubber), permitting the transmission of speech over a distance.

"But if we're beaten on it—" suggested the chief. "But I don't think that is possible. If there were any story to print, Dwyer would have had it here before now."

The managing editor looked steadily down at the floor.

"Very well," he said, slowly, "we won't wait any longer. Go ahead," he added, turning to the foreman with a sigh of reluctance. The foreman whirled himself about, and began to give his orders; but the two editors still looked at each other doubtfully.

As they stood so, there came a sudden shout and the sound of people running to and fro in the reportorial rooms below. There was the tramp of many footsteps on the stairs, and above the confusion they heard the voice of the city editor telling some one to "run to Madden's and get some brandy, quick."

No one in the composing-room said anything; but those compositors who had started to go home began slipping off their overcoats, and every one stood with his eyes fixed on the door.

It was kicked open from the outside, and in the doorway stood a cab-driver and the city editor, supporting between them a pitiful little figure of a boy, wet and miserable, and with the snow melting on his clothes and running in little pools to the floor. "Why, it's Gallegher," said the night editor, in a tone of the keenest disappointment.

Gallegher shook himself free from his supporters, and took an unsteady step forward, his fingers fumbling stiffly with the buttons of his waistcoat.

"Mr. Dwyer, sir," he began faintly, with his eyes fixed fearfully on the managing editor, "he got arrested—and I couldn't get here no sooner, 'cause they kept a-stopping me, and they took me cab from under me—but—" he pulled the notebook from his breast and held it out with its covers damp and limp from the rain, "but we got Hade, and here's Mr. Dwyer's copy."

And then he asked, with a queer note in his voice, partly of dread and partly of hope, "Am I in time, sir?"

The managing editor took the book, and tossed it to the foreman, who ripped out its leaves and dealt them out to his men as rapidly as a gambler deals out cards.

Then the managing editor stooped and picked Gallegher up in his arms, and, sitting down, began to unlace his wet and muddy shoes.

Gallegher made a faint effort to resist this degradation of the managerial dignity; but his protest was a very feeble one, and his head fell back heavily on the managing editor's shoulder.

To Gallegher the incandescent lights began to whirl about in circles, and to burn in different colors; the faces of the reporters kneeling before him and chafing his hands and feet grew dim and unfamiliar, and the roar and rumble of the great presses in the basement sounded far away, like the murmur of the sea.

And then the place and the circumstances of it came back to him again sharply and with sudden vividness.

Gallegher looked up, with a faint smile, into the managing editor's face. "You won't turn me off for running away, will you?" he whispered.

The managing editor did not answer immediately. His head was bent, and he was thinking, for some reason or other, of a little boy of his own, at home in bed. Then he said, quietly, "Not this time, Gallegher."

Gallegher's head sank back comfortably on the older man's shoulder, and he smiled comprehensively at the faces of the young men crowded around him. "You hadn't ought to," he said, with a touch of his old impudence, "'cause—I beat the town."

READING GROUP GUIDE

1. Did you guess the ending of *In the Fog*? If so, what tipped you off?

2. Did you have a theory of the murders?

3. Have you ever had an adventure as a result of getting lost?

4. Does *In the Fog* feel like it was written by an American author?

5. Did these stories make you want to read more by Davis? More stories about London? Or about boxing?

6. "Gallegher" and *In the Fog* are both called "crime fiction," yet they couldn't be more different. Which style appeals to you more? Why?

FURTHER READING

BY RICHARD HARDING DAVIS

Selected Fiction
Gallegher, and Other Stories. New York: Charles Scribner's Sons, 1891.

Van Bibber, and Others. New York: Harper & Bros., 1892.

The Exiles, and Other Stories. New York: Harper & Bros., 1894.

The Princess Aline. New York: Harper & Bros., 1895.

Soldiers of Fortune. New York: Charles Scribner's Sons, 1897.

Captain Macklin: His Memoirs. New York: Charles Scribner's Sons, 1902.

The Bar Sinister. New York: Charles Scribner's Sons, 1903.

The Scarlet Car. New York: Charles Scribner's Sons, 1907.

Once Upon a Time. New York: Charles Scribner's Sons, 1910.

The Lost Road. New York: Charles Scribner's Sons, 1913.

The Deserter. New York: Charles Scribner's Sons, 1917.

Selected Nonfiction
The West from a Car Window. New York: Harper & Bros., 1892.

Our English Cousins. New York: Harper & Bros., 1894.

Three Gringos in Venezuela and Central America. New York: Harper & Bros., 1896.

Cuba in War Time. New York: R. H. Russell, 1897.

A Year from a Reporter's Note-Book. New York: Harper & Bros., 1897.

The Cuban & Porto Rican Campaigns. New York: Charles Scribner's Sons, 1898.

With Both Armies in South Africa. New York: Charles Scribner's Sons, 1900. About the Second Boer War.

Real Soldiers of Fortune. New York: Charles Scribner's Sons, 1906. Collection of biographies.

Notes of a War Correspondent. New York: Charles Scribner's Sons, 1910.

With the Allies. New York: Charles Scribner's Sons, 1914.

With the French in France and Salonika. New York: Charles Scribner's Sons, 1916.

CRITICAL STUDIES

Corton, Christine L. *London Fog: The Biography.* Cambridge, MA and London: Belknap Press of Harvard University Press, 2015.

Downey, Fairfax. *Richard Harding Davis: His Day.* New York: Charles Scribner's Sons, 1933.

Langford, Gerald. *The Richard Harding Davis Years: A Biography of a Mother and a Son.* New York: Henry Holt, 1961.

Lubow, Arthur. *The Reporter Who Would Be King: A Biography of Richard Harding Davis.* New York: Scribner, 1992.

Miner, Lewis S. *Front Lines and Headlines: The Story of Richard Harding Davis.* New York: Julian Messner, 1959.

ABOUT THE AUTHOR

Richard Harding Davis, c. 1901. Photograph originally
copyrighted by Burr MacIntosh Studio. (Prints and
Photographs Division, Library of Congress)

Born in Philadelphia, Richard Harding Davis (1864–1916)
died just short of fifty-two years later, a little more than one
hundred miles to the northeast, in Mount Kisco, New York. In
the intervening years, Davis traveled around the world, experi-
encing romance, danger, war, and adventure.

Davis's father, Lemuel Clarke Davis, was the editor of the *Philadelphia Public Ledger*; his mother, Rebecca Harding Davis, was a well-known fiction writer. Family life was filled with celebrities of the stage as well as literary and visual artists. Davis was schooled at the Episcopal Academy in Philadelphia; then, after an unsatisfactory year at Swarthmore College, he enrolled at Lehigh University. College life was congenial, and Davis immediately took up writing for the student magazine. His first collection of short stories, *The Adventures of My Freshman*, largely drawn from his magazine work, appeared in 1884, when he was only twenty. After a postgraduate year at Johns Hopkins University, where he studied political economy, with his father's help, he landed a job at the *Philadelphia Record*. Dismissed from the *Record*, Davis had a brief stint at the *Philadelphia Press* before moving to the *New York Evening Sun* in 1888.

At the *Sun*, Davis soon shone. His picturesque style and coverage of controversial subjects such as abortion and suicide, as well as high-profile stories such as the Johnstown floods and the first electrocution of a criminal, brought attention to his writing. His first real success, however, was a story about a newsroom boy, Gallegher. Davis sold the story to *Scribner's Magazine* in March 1890 for the lofty sum of $175. When it was published in August 1890, he became an overnight success.* Later that year, he parlayed that triumph into employment as a managing editor of *Harper's Weekly* and began writing about his worldwide travels. This writing was collected in books such as *Rulers of the*

---

*The success of the story was crowned by the further success of Davis's collection *Gallegher, and Other Stories*, published in April 1891; the first edition sold out in a month, and an astonishing 15,346 copies were sold in the first year. Correspondence from Charles Scribner to Davis, cited in Arthur Lubow, *The Reporter Who Would Be King: A Biography of Richard Harding Davis* (New York: Charles Scribner's Sons, 1992), 80.

Mediterranean (1894), *About Paris* (1895), and *Three Gringos in Venezuela and Central America* (1896).

The work that would bring him international fame, however, was as a war correspondent. He reported on the Greco-Turkish War (April–May 1897) and, soon after, the Second Boer War (1899–1902), between the Boers and the English in South Africa. Subsequently, he would cover the Spanish-American War in Cuba (April–August 1898), sailing on a US Navy warship and embedding with the American troops. He was a good friend of Theodore Roosevelt and rode with the Rough Riders, even taking part in a raid and rescuing the wounded—for which efforts Roosevelt made him an honorary member. Later, he covered the Russo-Japanese War (1904–05) from the perspective of the Japanese troops. In the autumn of 1915, he was at the Salonika front in the First World War, but his unexpected death by angina pectoris six months later ended his coverage of the Great War.

Davis was also a prolific writer of fiction, both novels and short stories. Many were based on his personal experiences. *Soldiers of Fortune* (1897), *The King's Jackal* (1898), *Captain Macklin* (1902), and *The White Mice* (1909) all drew on his war stories, as did his nonfiction book of biographies, *Real Soldiers of Fortune* (1906). The latter included an early biography of Winston Churchill, whom Davis knew and admired. His short stories filled ten volumes; he also penned about two dozen plays, some of which were based on his own works, some original.

Davis's personal life was as dramatic as his adventurous career. He married first, in 1899, an artist named Cecil Clark. He had known Cecil since she was a young girl—their families were friends and neighbors during summer holidays. Davis spent two years courting Cecil, even portraying her in a book. In *The Lion and the Unicorn*, Helen Cabot, a beautiful

American portrait painter, is courted by a handsome American playwright, Philip Carroll, whom she has known since her teens. Carroll has come to London to have a play produced and is delighted to find Cabot there as well. Though she has rebuffed Carroll's numerous proposals, in the end, when Carroll despairs and plans to leave London, Cabot relents. So too, Cecil finally was persuaded to marry Davis. The wedding was a grand affair, the wedding party including Davis's friends, actress Ethel Barrymore and illustrator Charles Dana Gibson.*

The marriage was a curious one: "platonic" was the description applied by some friends. "We will simply be as brother and sister," Cecil reportedly told Davis.† Perhaps inevitably, Davis fell in love with another woman, an actress and vaudeville performer named Bessie McCoy (real name Elizabeth Genevieve McEvoy). Born and bred in vaudeville, McCoy achieved wide popularity in 1908 for her "Yama Yama Man" routine, a wild song and dance about a boogeyman. Davis was entranced by her performance and eventually won an introduction to her. A long courtship by correspondence followed.

Meanwhile, Davis's mother, Rebecca, with whom he was extremely close, was quite ill. Davis wrote her virtually every day that they were not together, but now the end was near. Davis had not told her of the fissure in his marriage, and divorce still carried a stigma. After Rebecca died in 1910, however, Cecil filed for divorce, though it was not finalized until 1912. Three weeks later, Davis married Bessie. Twice her age and set in his ways, Davis took charge of his wife and forbade her any further

---

*Gibson and Davis met in London in July 1889. Davis posed for Gibson for the cover of the humor magazine *Life*, and Gibson subsequently illustrated Davis's *Gallegher, and Other Stories*, published in 1891 (Lubow, 68).

†The source is a column by Chester R. Hope titled "Curious Kink in 'Dickie' Davis' Character," *Cleveland Leader*, May 7, 1916, quoted in Lubow, 202.

dancing. Soon, however, came what Davis called "the Blessing." On January 4, 1915, Bessie gave birth to a daughter, whom they named Hope, after the heroine of Davis's most popular novel, *Soldiers of Fortune*. Davis rejoiced in the child and took great pleasure in her company. Sadly, he would share her company for only a year. Davis died at his desk, on the telephone, of heart failure on April 11, 1916.

As popular as his writing was, it was his personality that caught the public's attention. It is true, observed Arthur Lubow in *The Reporter Who Would Be King: A Biography of Richard Harding Davis*, that "Davis reported on wars and other great events; he wrote best-selling fiction and his plays. But all of that is beside the central point. Davis sparked the fantasies of a generation of Americans. Boys and young men dreamed of becoming him, girls and young women imagined marrying him. They were enraptured by the image of a well-bred, handsome, clean-living man who was equally at home at a dinner party or on a battlefield. In both his life and his fiction, Davis consciously created that image."* As perhaps the ultimate step in creating that image, Davis posed for Gibson, who portrayed Davis as the ideal companion for the "Gibson girl," a paradigm of female beauty in the era.

Despite the tremendous contemporary popularity of the man and his work, Davis's writing was later dismissed as "smart and shallow" by critic Ludwig Lewisohn.† "Like many handsome and idolized American college men, he never quite graduated," judged Francis Hackett in 1918.‡ Others came to appreciate his work. In a lavish seven-page spread in the October 11, 1924,

---

*Lubow, 3.

---

†*Expression in America* (New York: Harper & Bros., 1932), 85.

‡"Richard Harding Davis," *New Republic*, March 2, 1918, 150 (a review of *The Adventures and Letters of Richard Harding Davis* by Charles Belmont Davis).

issue of *Liberty*, with numerous photographs of Davis in the company of various celebrities of the day, Thomas Beer heaped praise on Davis. The article was headed "Richard Harding Davis, whose works preserve for all ages the adventurous, expansionist spirit of the decades that ushered in the twentieth century, the world war, and our own times."*

Today, critics' judgment of Davis's work is mixed. According to scholar Clayton L. Eichelberger, "Critics have often claimed that [he] failed as a writer of fiction because he excelled as a journalist." But Eichelberger disputes that judgment: "Davis incorporated in his fiction the best qualities of his journalism— his quick recognition of the picturesque, his unerring selection of interest-arousing features, his keen eye for external detail, his easy phrasing of remarkably lively impressionist passages, his youthful appreciation of adventure and movement."†

Just as his image entranced millions, so too do Richard Harding Davis's life and writing reflect the popular spirit of the decades of the late nineteenth and early twentieth centuries. Seen through Davis's eyes, a time of war and hardship became an exhilarating and romantic adventure.

**Liberty, October 11, 1924, 15. The editors puffed the piece with the following summation: "A Man to Be Remembered. To the young men and boys of the period in which he wrote, Richard Harding Davis was an inspiration. And even today his writings are a stimulating influence. Despite the lapse of years, his books are among the best sellers, always absorbing, ever realistic. His characters breathe the breath of life, for Davis lived his characters" (16). Beer himself was lauded by the editors as "the most promising of young American writers." Though he was a prolific writer and widely read in the 1920s and 1930s, today he is remembered, if at all, only for his biography of Stephen Crane.

†Clayton L. Eichelberger, "Richard Harding Davis: Overview," *Reference Guide to American Literature*, ed. by Jim Kamp, 3rd ed. (London: St. James Press, 1994). *Gale Literature Resource Center*, link.gale.com/apps/doc/H1420002131 /LitRC?u=lapl&sid=bookmark-LitRC&xid=f8d541fb.